Marking my Men

Bink Cummings

BINK CUMMINGS

Copyright © 2018 by: Bink Cummings
ISBN: **978-1718875043**

All rights reserved. No part of this book may be reproduced or transmitted in any form or by any means, electronic or mechanical, including photocopying, recording or by any information storage and retrieval system, without written permission from the author, except for the inclusion of brief quotations in a review.
Proofreader/Editor- Mary Bevinger & Judy Zweifel
Proofreader/Beta- Heather Hendrickson
Cover Designer- Bink Cummings
Photo provided from: Big Stock

This book doesn't represent BDSM lifestyles as a whole. Only a small piece of the world that is oftentimes misunderstood.
Remember to practice- safe, sane, and consensual sex, in all forms.

To Deb, the initiator of this massive kink fest. Marking My Men would've never been possible without your wild imagination first drilling the idea into mine.
You created a monster of filthy proportions.
Thanks for being you.

BINK CUMMINGS

1

MEET THE MISTRESS

"My milkshake brings all the naughty subs to my yard," I belt my own lyrical rendition at the top of my lungs, swiveling my wide hips to the beat in a black lace thong, and simple spaghetti strap tank top. It's cleaning day, for now. In about an hour I get to meet up with one of my most favorite people in the entire world. I'm giddy with anticipation.

Shoving a piece of onyx-colored hair out of my face; I pull the freshly laundered roleplay garments from my dryer, and rest the heaping pile on top to hang. To avoid wrinkles, I have to do it right away. The French maid costume is a pain in the ass to keep crisp. With my luck, I'll have to iron the ruffles this time. The slutty nurse outfit isn't much better. You don't realize how tedious caring for fetish wear is until you have to wash it twice a week. Faux leather and latex outfits are done by hand, as is lace. Then they hang to dry in my spacious laundry room. I had this area gutted and expanded five years ago to service all my needs in one central location. The biggest addition was the stainless steel sink with marble countertop on the opposite side of where my washer and dryer sit. There's a wall of cupboards above it that houses all sorts of kinky stuff. I also had them build a closet to store typical household cleaning tools, like my mop, broom, and vacuum. The bright Playboy Bunny pink walls are my favorite part, aside from the drawer dishwasher under the counter. I know a dishwasher in your laundry room, weird, right? Not for me. Where else do you clean dildos and butt plugs? In your kitchen dishwasher? By hand? Over my dead body. It's hard enough scrubbing dried cum from lace. Sanitizing sex toys I leave to the machines, for the most part, but those damn vibes have to be done by hand. Another thing I'm not fond of. But it's part of the job description.

Twirling on my tippy toes, shakin' what my mama gave me, I separate the need-to-fold from the need-to-hang garments.

I guess this is the portion of our introduction where I say "Hi," like we're in an AA meeting, then confess I'm a sex worker. *Pish posh.* Don't you even think for one second that I'm a prostitute, I'm not. I'm what people in my industry call a ProDomme. In simpler terms, a professional mistress. Basically, I fulfill men's deepest, filthiest, dick-rubbing fantasies without engaging in sex. We explore kinks most men are too afraid to admit to anyone besides themselves. That's where I come in. To free their wily ways, so to speak.

If you're a guy who wants to dress up as a maid and be spanked with a wooden spoon 'til you come your brains out, I'm your woman. If you hate your peen so much you tape it between your legs and need to punish it with a flogger, I'm the one you give a ring-a-ding. Want to roll around in garlic buttered noodles dressed up as a slutty chef? Need to be spanked by a high heel while a plug vibrates in your pert little bum? How about tied to a St. Andrew's Cross while I pour hot wax down your body and recite verses from the Bible in a seductive tone? If you have a penis and any portion of what I mentioned gets you horny, then I'm your gal—Mistress Ronan, if you wanna get technical. Anything less respectful and I'll see you under my boot heel.

Full disclosure, those scenes are merely the tippy top of the iceberg where my job is concerned. I bet you're wondering, did you really do all those crazy things? The answer is hell yes. Sometimes more than once. For reference, soy candles are the way to go during play. They have a lower melting point and are easier to remove from chest hair. You know, in case you're ever in the mood to experiment.

Belting out the last verse of *Milkshake*, I shake out the maid costume that a client donned yesterday, slip it onto a hanger, and hook it on one of the two fancy ladders suspended from the ceiling. The idea to use these as drying racks came from Pinterest. What a nifty site that is. Next, I shake out a pair of cotton pleasure shorts and fold them into fourths. I love these wannabe boxers. They're the simplest way to let your submissive dress up while keeping their dick and asshole readily available. That's imperative in my dungeon. I tend to have a lot of clients who crave anal play. More so than friends of mine who are also in the business. I must attract those type of guys. Not that I mind. Prostate stimulation is mighty fun. You've never truly lived until you've had a man sob to come when you're pegging his man-g and nothing else. It's the ultimate power. Not to mention it makes me super wet—like Niagara Falls.

Before we go any further, I feel it's necessary I dispel any sort of bullshit misconceptions you might have about my profession. First and foremost, you need to understand that this *is* a job. Where you might go to the office every day to your boring desk job, *no offense*, I go to my basement. Which I converted into the dungeon of my dreams eight years ago, complete with a separate entrance. I work set hours. My potential clients fill out applications to be considered a submissive. I conduct interviews with each candidate before accepting them as a client. Yes, I might fulfill men's desires, or act as a quasi-therapist for $300 an hour. But I don't give blowjobs, have sex with clients in any capacity, or allow them to touch me above the knee. Ready to quit your job and become a ProDomme yet? All of my toys, aside from plugs, are covered in condoms when in use—safety first. The plugs themselves are client owned, and I have individual boxes for each one. That trusty label maker has to come in handy sometime. At the core of it all... every single thing we do is safe, sane, and one hundred percent consensual. Right down to the jelly-filled donuts men like to eat off my toes. They *are* kinda cute—my toes. Not that I'm into foot fetishes myself.

Finishing the laundry, another upbeat song blares through my speakers as I dance, sing, and let loose until the task is complete. Then I go about the handful of other things I need done before Tyler arrives. The colorful array of dildos are removed from the dishwasher and placed in a wire basket that my assistant uses to carry them down to the basement. My dungeon isn't a single large space like one might think. It's split into various fetish rooms that all serve different purposes. Kendra, my loyal, albeit feisty assistant, who books my appointments alongside performing maid duties, is the cornerstone of my operation. She oversees the scenes, prepares for them ahead of time, even wipes up the cum mess afterward. She's worth every penny I pay her, and then some.

By the time I've completed the necessary duties one must tolerate when running your own kink-based business, I head to my bedroom that's way down yonder in my 1950s brick ranch, here in good ole Charlotteton, Kentucky. Half of my mansion-quality walk-in closet houses what I refer to as my street clothes, the other half is where my play garb hangs. For Tyler, I select a pair of black thigh-highs that have a stripe up the back and bow adorning the top. They pair nicely with my black, bandage-style bustier, complete with strappy neckline, built-in garter straps, and O-ring details for an overall saucy dominatrix vibe. To finish off the look, I slip on a sheer, crotchless thong. For my usual clients, I wear entirely different attire that encompasses the stereotypical Mistress feel—leather, vinyl, corsets, and thigh-high boots. Tonight, I opt for simple black pumps. They're Tyler's favorite, thus making them a favorite of mine.

In the bathroom, I remove my old-school Caboodle of makeup from the cupboard and paint my face on. Red lips, black coal around my hazel eyes, smoky eyeshadow, falsies, and gloss to make my lips gleam under the dim lights of the dungeon. Untying my long, black hair, I comb my fingers through the unruly curls to tame them. It's pointless. They never want to comply. To make them yield, I apply hair product to my palms and work it through the thick strands. Brushes do nothing but worsen the curls, so I try to avoid them at all costs. When I'm satisfied with the results, I sweep my fingers into the top of my head and begin the task of French braiding this wild beast of mine.

"Ronan." Kendra pokes her head into the bathroom.

"Yeah?" I meet her gaze through the mirror above my double vanity.

She leans a shoulder against the doorjamb, arms tucked loosely across her perky breasts. "He's here."

Hanging my head, I grip the marble top and take a deep breath, willing my heart *not* to go berserk. A pointless endeavor on my part. The heart wants what it wants, and Tyler is hers, through and through. Half faithful to him, the other to Rob—the two men who make up my entire world, beyond job, reason, or mundane life. They're my better halves. The two souls on this planet who've bonded with mine. Five years ago, I would've said falling in love was impossible. That is... until Rob came into my life. Two years after, Tyler fell into our life, fitting seamlessly. Now's not the time to go over this *thing* we share. He's here, in my house, and I'm already growing wet at the mere thought. Damn, my pulse is thrumming. Mouth salivating. I cannot wait to see him, even if I have to pretend I'm not overjoyed by his presence.

Another cleansing breath in and out before the Domme veil drops over my face. "Already?" I ask, tone casual. Kendra can see straight through my façade. We've been friends long enough. My composure isn't for her, though. It's for me to keep a clear mind. Being a giddy schoolgirl doesn't work well for what I'm about to do.

"He's only ten minutes early. That's better than last week," she supplies, pretending she doesn't see my inner struggle. I adore her for that.

Tyler was an hour early last Monday. He got the flogging of his life for it, too. Rules are rules. If you don't obey your Mistress's word, you get punished. Not that I mind my man being a bit overeager to see me. It's flattering as hell. Still, my rules are not meant to be broken. You toe the line or suffer the consequences.

"Did he—"

"*Closer* is already playing," she cuts in.

"Is he—"

"Yes. Naked."

"Did you—"

"You know I wouldn't do that."

Right. Duh. I know she wouldn't, but that doesn't stop me from asking. Anyone seeing my man nude besides me, as illogical as it sounds, makes me itch to mark him. To brand his perfect pale skin for all to see. I know he already bears the marks of our love every single day. Ones that are special to only us. But the deep, almost seductive craving to mar him shoots fire through my veins. My fingers twitch in anticipation. Pussy, desperate for release.

Tyler isn't like other clients. He's not really a client at all. He's *my* submissive. The rules do not apply to him. None of them do. Aside from the most basic

one—that I'm his Domme and he's *mine*.
It's time to play.

2

THE ARTISTRY OF MASCOCHISM

Sauntering up the dimly lit hallway of my dungeon, as the solid *click-click* of my heels resonate underfoot, I mentally prepare for our session. Tyler is unlike anyone I've met before. Not only is he gorgeous inside and out, he's nine years my junior, a world-renowned artist, and... deaf. That's why his playlist of rock music rattles the walls, the seductive pulse threading its way through your skin, claiming your heartbeat. He needs to *feel* the inflections since he can't hear it.

I poise my hand on the cool knob, forming my fingers around the brass. Behind the door is our place. The room I share only with Tyler and Rob, no one else. Here is where the music resides. Where bonds are formed. Inside, will be Tyler, naked and waiting, his cock hard. Although we can speak back and forth like you and me, words will not be spoken in our place. Tyler's lip-reading is second to none. But there will be no need for that, either. Sign is our language of love when in session. Three years ago when I first met the fun, enthusiastic man I fell for, the barrier between the hearing and deaf didn't really exist. If he didn't have a habit of signing alongside his talking, you couldn't tell the man before you was any different. So, for a while, that's how we played. Learning each other's nuances. Until I needed more. Six months into our S&M relationship, I started taking night classes to learn ASL. Thanks to that, along with Tyler's help, I've become fluent in sign. In my humble opinion, it's that extra step that brought us closer and subsequently together as a couple, no longer client and ProDomme, but lovers in the purest form.

Shoulders pushed back, I adjust my average boobs for optimal oomph, wiggle my toes inside these heels to center myself, and enter our kinkdom. Not wanting Tyler to discern my enthusiasm, my expression remains neutral as I slowly take in the room, not the body standing in the middle. The recessed lighting overhead provides ideal ambiance, illuminating sporadic spotlights on the hardwood floor. They are perfect to place your sub in should you wish to watch them perform. The brightness blinds their ability to see you well, much like an actor on stage. The heather-gray walls are romantic. Yet, the variety of instruments hanging from floor to ceiling on one wall illustrates the room's purpose. Cat o' nine tails, whips, floggers, paddles, shackles, among many other tools of my trade are purposely hung in plain view—meant to entice my men, not scare them into submission. The black St. Andrew's Cross serves as the focal point of the space. I eye the top half above Tyler's head, refusing to reward him with a direct perusal of his form. Like any good sub, he has to wait. In the furthest corner is a plush, velvet chair with arms. I call it my throne—the perfect spot for my men to worship me. Across from it is Tyler's makeshift painting studio, complete with easel and small cart for his essentials. You'll see why this matters later. On the opposite side of the room, closest to where I stand, is a matte black, four-poster bed. Evidently, Kendra decided red silk sheets were ideal for tonight's events, and I couldn't agree more. I'm wet just imagining what's to come.

One leisurely step at a time, I enter and shut the door with seductive grace. My back to Tyler, I run both palms down the front of my not-so-flat stomach, wicking away the sweat that's gathered on them. This is not a job where you can be self-conscious about your body. You either embrace what you have, or you fake it. I do a bit of both. My mama didn't give me model good looks, height, or a lithe body. The last time I saw single digits in clothing sizes was in middle school. Sure, I might not have stretch marks, but I have a spot or two of cellulite. I'm painfully average in height, coming in at five foot five barefoot. In the world of Judgey McJudgersons, my body type would be considered pear. These hips and ass are what my submissives call luscious. At least the two that are mine do. And that's good enough for me. Life's too short to worry about body composition. Some women are lucky to be hourglasses, while I'm over here rockin' junk in the trunk with a pair of grapefruits to keep me company up top. It could be worse.

Expelling a rushed breath, I briefly close my eyes and willfully uncage the rabid depravity from my inner sanctum. It's at the deepest part of me that I keep hidden on a daily basis. The dirtiest pieces of my soul. The ones that latched on to Tyler during our first session, recognizing him as a kindred spirit. I may not be a sadist at heart, but there's part of me that craves something as equally addictive—marking. To see what my mastery has inflicted gives me the greatest pleasure. To have a man proudly wear my brand is the highest of highs. So I must prepare myself to view the gift of marred flesh that Tyler carries from our last scene.

The final pulse of *More Human than Human* by White Zombie fades out. I squeeze my thighs together and revel in the zing that radiates there. My heartbeat pounds in my chest. Fingertips itch to touch. One final respiration and I'm ready to be me, without fear of rejection or guilt. It took years to accept this corrupt part of myself. Every day it's a struggle. That's what makes my job perfect. It gives me the outlet I need to stay sane. Being with Tyler and Rob goes beyond that. To something I'd call divine.

Turning around to face him, my eyes scan Tyler's glorious body. As promised, he's hard, so very hard as he stares straight ahead. None of that kneeling nonsense for my men. They stand because I respect them. They obey because they respect me. His ice-blue eyes widen as he takes in my outfit from head to toe. Gaze landing on the swell of my breasts, the smallest, almost shy grin tugs at the corner of his mouth. *Compliment received.* He approves. If that's not indication enough, the slow sweep of Tyler's tongue across his full bottom lip cements his appreciation. Suppressing a shiver, I watch a thin stream of pre-cum cascade from his pierced slit onto the floor. His cock bobs there, performing for its mate. Tyler's putting on a show for me. One that we're both aware of, but don't acknowledge. He wants to entice his Mistress and is doing a damn fine job of it.

My mouth begins to water as he flexes that dick again, sending a stream of pre-cum flying, catching the light just right. Tyler's member is a masterpiece much like the man himself. It's the perfect thickness; a virile seven inches that he's decorated with jewelry from crown to base. A chunky Prince Albert hoop loops through the head. Along the underside is an eight-rung Jacobs latter. I'm not sure which I like more. They're both a turn-on.

Without addressing him, I let the music carry my steps to the wall of tools. Unhooking two leashes from their designated spots, I make sure he can see what I'm doing. Anticipation is half the excitement. Pivoting on my heel, I approach Tyler and stop three feet away—so close yet so far. Poised to keep my excitement in check, I drape both leashes over my forearm a few inches apart. One is medium-weight leather, the other lighter nylon; both sufficient for our use. Gesturing toward them with the subtle jut of my chin, I give him the option to pick his desired heft. What he chooses will determine how deep we go tonight.

Aware he's not allowed to touch me without permission, he quickly points to the leather before returning the arm to his side.

Hmmm. Perfect.

He wants it hard. I was hoping for the same as well.

Pleased, I grin inwardly at the prospect. Tonight's

gonna be fun.

Making him wait a tad bit longer, I return the nylon leash to its place. Then it's show time. Leather clasped in one hand, I wrap my fist around his erection with the other. His pulse throbs through my palm, the heat of his flesh warming my chilly fingers from the outside in. Stroking him roughly, *once, twice*, a series of severe tremors wrack Tyler's frame. I draw another bubble of pre-cum from the tip. *That's it, baby, take the pleasure.* Opening the metal clasp of the leash, I connect it to his Prince Albert and let go of everything. Tyler's throat works through thick swallows, lips slightly parted. His six-pack flexing, the leather falls into a heap at his feet, forcing his cock to point downward, drawing the skin taut at his smooth pubis. Damn, that's sexy. *He's* sexy. Even the bareness he favors, apart from his legs that're covered in a dark smattering of hair, is sexy. It makes his dick look bigger. Engorged even; with all the blood flowing south from the leather weighing it down. Excited, my pussy clenches at the decadent sight before me, and my gums begin to ache.

I need to bite him.

To sink my teeth into the side of his neck. Into his collarbones.

The hickies there are starting to heal. That's unacceptable.

Closing my eyes, giving myself a mental shake, I beat the overwhelming desire down with a baseball bat. My tongue runs across the front of my teeth. I nibble my bottom lip. There's no need to get ahead of ourselves. He'll be well used by the time the night's through.

Soaking up my fill before we get started, I circle Tyler slowly, appraising him like a prized bull. This too heightens the anticipation tenfold. The tiny shuffle of his feet is an adorable tell. Pausing to ogle his backside, I groan under my breath at the view. As I suspected, his firm ass cheeks are a thing of beauty, covered in yellowish bruises from our mild paddle session. Leftover love bites are still imprinted across the expanse of his shoulder blades. Satisfied by the marks, I slowly draw a finger down Tyler's curved spine. He shivers, goosebumps flaring to the surface. I grin. There's just something about his pure, creamy white skin that's extra fun to mar. It reddens beautifully.

Drawing my fingertip to the base of Tyler's tailbone, I dip between his cleft to tease his backdoor. His cheeks clench, locking my digit in place, then loosen just as quickly when he recognizes the intent. My man's a magnificent bottom. Loves to be fucked. Hungry for it, even. I consider it an honor to watch him fall apart on my cock.

Brushing over his hole, that's slick with lube per my instructions, I trace around the rim on tormenting repeat, revving his libido. He pushes his bottom back, seeking more. Smiling at his eagerness, I give him a small taste by dipping the tiniest fraction inside, feeling his muscles squeeze around the invader. Jesus, he has a sexy ass. Look at how much he wants me in there. And people wonder why this is highly addictive. Why I need it as much as my personal subs do. The appetite for pleasure-laced pain that vibrates throughout Tyler is so heady, I can almost smell its sweet aroma. That's why he's mine.

Why this space is ours. Why I don't jump straight into the whips. Tyler's like an aged cognac, you savor every taste. You don't chug him down like a cheap beer at a frat party.

Hands fisted at his sides, Tyler gifts me yet another hug from his hole, as it envelops the pad of my finger. Impatient to get the ball rolling, he tries his luck, and pushes back on my digit, urging it deeper. But I stop him with a sharp smack on the ass. Agitated that he's letting his baser needs rule, I *tsk* aloud even though he can't hear me.

Naughty, naughty man needs to be taught a lesson.

Nobody rushes my perfection. Most of all him.

If I want to take things slow, I'll take them slow. If I want to pull out my strap-on, bend him over, and make him my slut, I will. The darn masochist can't hold his stinking horses.

Placing a foot between Tyler's, I kick his legs apart to widen his stance. He complies way too eagerly. Then I reach between his thighs, careful not to touch his cock, and grab the leash, pulling it backward. He rewards me with a guttural moan that registers a few decibels above *NIN*.

Extracting my finger from his passage, I tease his smooth pucker before grasping the leather and using the handle to paddle his butt. Three quick slaps on each cheek is plenty reprimand for now. Any more and he'll start his initial descent into subspace. It doesn't take much to get him to skim the surface. It's reaching the bottom of the abyss that takes patience.

Ah yes, this is the hors d'oeuvre course of the evening.

To drive Tyler crazier, I spread his cheek with one hand and rub the leash over his hole with the other. A puddle of pre-cum gathers between his feet as I yank on his dick, forcing it between his legs. Not that he minds. Tyler has a safe word of sorts—a special sign. One he's never used to stop a scene. If I wanted to bend his cock back and make him fuck his own asshole, he'd let me. Perhaps that's something I should consider another day.

My artist's chin drops to his chest as I abrade his rim. His shoulders begin to shake between passes. Another moan erupts from his throat. I spank him with the leash again, harder this time, and return to tormenting his asshole. Back and forth, I swap from spanking to abusing his entry. Broken cries begin to pour like rich molasses. I grip his cheek, watching my nails bite into flesh.

Toes curling in my heels, I shudder with power, loving this far too much already.

Slap. My palm joins in on the fun.

Firm skin bounces under my assault as pinkness blooms. My pussy grows wetter. A thin sheen of sweat coats Tyler's back.

Ousting a heavy breath, I force myself to stop. If I don't, that leather will end up fucking his hole, and my teeth will embed in his bottom.

I take a careful step back and drop the leash. Then watch in rapt fascination as Tyler trembles from head to toe without me laying a single finger on him.

What a beautiful, beautiful man.

The slender cut of his body is not something I thought I'd find attractive. Yet, do. He has the arms and shoulders of an artist. Hours of paint strokes have carved muscle so precise, like a sculptor with his clay. Add in a killer metabolism, and you get Tyler—a five-foot-ten, masochistic artist with a heart the size of a whale and a sunny disposition.

Now it's time for the salad course.

Circling back around, I grip Tyler's chin between my thumb and forefinger to garner eye contact.

Oh, sweet mercy, he's already wrecked. His lips are swollen from biting them, blue eyes glassy, face flushed. He blinks slowly through hooded lids, watching me watch him.

Because I can't control it any longer, I wet my lips and lean in just enough to sweep my mouth across his in the barest of touches. The connection sparks, sending a tendril of hunger to my nipples and sex. I pull back before I dive in for a full-bodied taste. Instead, I wrap my fist around his velvet steel and close my eyes to concentrate on his pulse drumming against my skin. It centers me enough to do what needs to be done. When I'm with other men as their Domme, there's no need to control any urges, because there are none. I never get aroused or desire to kiss them. Being with Tyler takes discipline on my part, when an innocent touch means everything.

Needing a bit more, I press our bodies together. Folding his cock against my belly, I nuzzle his throat. Tyler smells amazing there. Like cologne, musk, and paint—a unique scent that could never be replicated by anyone but him. A rumble of contentment vibrates in his chest as I nibble down to his collarbone and lave my tongue across the protruding bone. If I wanted to, I could sip wine from the notch above his clavicle. To prove this theory, I dip my tongue into the shallow bowl. My masochist sputters on contact as I grin, loving the effect I have on him.

The ache in my gums intensifies.

Screw it.

Sinking my teeth into the side of his throat, I give in to temptation and fulfill both our needs at once. Moaning deep and ravenous, I extract fronds of depravity from the recesses of my soul, eyelids sliding shut. *Yes. That's it.* My tongue flicks the supple skin as I nibble it between my teeth. Tyler returns a moan even louder than my own, a violent shudder washing through him. The dick between us lurches. Then I feel it... hot jets of cum bathing my stomach. I groan, pussy clenching tight as he wastes his nut on us; not where it's supposed to be.

Well, well, well, isn't he full of surprises tonight? He knows the rules. No release until I say so. Somebody's in trouble.

Refusing to give him any more marks, for now, I step back, separating us and the sticky cum mess that coats our bellies.

Furrowing my brows so he can tell that I'm displeased, I swipe the back of my hand across my lips to clear the saliva there.

"*You came*," I sign, tapping my foot on the ground in annoyance. In truth, I'm not that upset by it. I actually find it kinda sexy he couldn't control himself for once. But, I can't show that. You break the rules, you face my wrath.

Tyler bows his head in shame, a piece of his faux hawk falling onto his forehead. "*I'm sorry, Mistress.*"

"*Why did you come?*"

Tears gather in the corner of his eyes, bottom lip

wobbling. *"It's been three days."*

"Three days since what?"

Tyler shuffles from foot to foot. *"I was here."*

"That's your excuse?"

"You know I don't... You know." His fingers trail off.

"Come without me?"

He nods, crestfallen. If I wasn't his Domme, I'd wrap him in a hug to wash that horrible expression off his face.

I never said Tyler couldn't ejaculate without me present. It's a choice he made on his own. One I've never held him to.

By Tyler's bizarre anxiousness and his impatience with our session tonight, something tells me there's more to this than he's letting on. Perhaps he met someone else. It's always a possibility. We don't exactly have a normal relationship. Then again, he'd be upfront about that. The only thing in his life he's reluctant to speak about is his art. Pain is Tyler's muse. It's the driving force behind his masterpieces. Very few know this about him. None of the articles written about him reveal his kink. When he first applied to be a submissive, I noticed right away he was trying to fulfill his masochistic needs with self-infliction. Penile and testicular torture to be exact. He initially got his piercings as a way to extract the level of pain he needs, to see whatever he sees inside that brilliant head of his. During our first exam, his cockhead was puffy and red, the slit almost swollen shut, balls well beyond their usual size. During our long talk, he admitted that he'd tried everything from tying rubber bands around his balls to hitting his dick with a mallet.

This most definitely has to do with his art.

"*What color?*" I prompt, referring to the subby high color chart we devised a month after our first session all those years ago. When you work with a deaf man, and there's music pulsing through the room, words are impossible to discern. That's why we invented a way to understand highs without speech. Each color is given a value and a sign, which is nothing more than the first letter of the word. At base level Tyler is white or W. Then goes the subsequent colors yellow, orange, red, green, blue, purple, silver, and gold.

"*Gold,*" he signs in return.

I was right.

This is serious.

"*To gold?*" I verify, taken aback.

"*Yes.*"

"*For how long?*"

"*All night.*"

That's not good.

"*You're having trouble with painting this week. Aren't you?*"

Tyler nods, bottom lip pulled between his teeth.

"*Why, sweetheart?*"

"*You know why.*"

Arching an inquisitive brow, I wait for him to elaborate. He knows I won't stand for evasive answers.

"*You. Me. Rob.*"

"*What about us?*"

"*It's time, Mistress. Two days a week for us both isn't enough.*"

My stomach dips at his directness. Heat pooling there as a kaleidoscope of butterflies breaks free.

I swallow the sudden knot in my throat.

"Have you spoken to Rob?"

"Yes. Sort of."

"I don't know if I'm ready."

Tyler's not buying my bullcrap for a second. *"You are. We all are. It was always gonna come to this, Mistress."*

He's right. I dunno why I've been reluctant to make us more permanent. Change can be difficult. In this case, it's scary. What if we can't be this way every day? What if it's just a fantasy?

Enough.

I shake my head, ridding it of such thoughts. I can deal with that later. We're in session now.

'That still doesn't explain why you came." I revert back to the topic at hand.

"I've been hard, a lot, thinking about you this week. I couldn't wait to be here. I need you to take me to gold. All night long."

"I can't take you to gold again for another month if that's what you want."

This is going to be rough on the both of us. My muscles will be screaming for days.

A firm nod. *"I do."*

"You'll hurt for a week, if not longer." Our typical sessions hover around red or green on the subby high chart. The last time I took Tyler to gold I had to improvise on client domination for a week. Wielding a simple paddle was impossible. My assistant even had to help dress me. It was one of the best sessions of my life. One that's marked my soul forever.

Fingers moving in sharp, fluid-like grace, Tyler explains himself. *"I know. I need to feel you on me for a week. When I sit down, I need to feel you. When I touch my neck, I need to feel you. The effects of the paddling this week lasted a day, then I couldn't feel you anymore. I fucking hate that."*

"You need to feel me?" God, why is it so hot watching him admit that?

"Every single day. I need to feel you on my skin, under it."

My heart flutters.

"Gold is asking a lot, sweetie."

Pursing his lips together to fight off a smile, Tyler tilts his head to the side, eyeing me like I'm a big fat fibber. *"No, it's not. You're afraid you'll like it too much. That you won't be able to let me leave after it's over."*

I sigh inwardly. I'm not supposed to be that transparent. He isn't supposed to be able to read me like I do him.

"You can't know that."

"But, I do. I'm yours. You're mine. I need gold, Mistress. Then I need to paint for you." His hardening cock flexes as he signs, still weighed down by the leash hanging from the tip, where remnants of cum reside.

Sheesh, I love that dick. But what I love just as much is when Tyler paints for me. There's always a canvas ready for him on the easel, waiting to be touched. Watching him work is like witnessing firsthand a modern day Dali, or William Blake transform nothing special into something extraordinary. There's a reason why many of his originals sell for hundreds of thousands of dollars. If he had sold the twelve originals I have decorating my walls upstairs, he'd be wealthy beyond my wildest imagination. That is, if Tyler cared about money. He doesn't. That's why he wears paint-splattered Converse and holey jeans everywhere. I find it, along with everything else about him, charming.

"You want me to keep you at gold through the entire painting?"

He nods twice, dark hair flopping every which way, affirming what I feared.

This is going to be a long, pleasurable, soul-altering night.

It's moments like this I wish I didn't need him as much as I do.

If I don't break down by the end of the session, it'll be a miracle. Hurting him like he wants, not only wears me out physically, it rips open my chest cavity for him to see the soft gooey parts inside. A place I protect for my own peace of mind.

Resolving myself to the unknown, I reply, *"If gold is the level you want, I'll get you there."*

Tyler bows his head in gratitude, a happy smirk hooking the corner of his full mouth. *"Thank you, Mistress."*

"You're most welcome." I return a bright smile, willing my heart not to beat itself out of my chest. I cannot believe I agreed to this. The last time we reached gold, I held him for hours, stroking his sweaty hair, as he shuddered through the aftermath of climax. That night he'd been allowed a single orgasm. He was a trooper through all that I put him through. Tonight, with his spend already coating my

front, I'll need to decide how many more climaxes he'll be permitted to have. Possibly none, since he already broke a cardinal rule.

"*I love you.*" Tyler blushes tomato red at his admission, one that neither of us takes lightly.

"*I love you way more. Now walk your sexy ass to the cross. It's time to punish you for coming without permission.*"

"*Yes, Mistress. Thank you for my punishment.*"

I snort at his politeness.

Damn masochists, always so darn eager.

It's time for the main course.

3

COLORS OF SUBMISSION

Spread eagle, back to me, tied to the St. Andrew's Cross, Tyler's sweat glistens beneath the overhead spotlight. Manson's *This is the New Shit* pounds through the speakers as the sharp crack of my bullwhip slashes across my lover's shoulders. His calves flex on impact, cheeks clenching tight. A moan resonates loud and husky, making me squirm. *That's it, baby. That's what I love to hear.* Tyler's coming apart, and we've barely gotten started. Angry red slash marks bloom in crisscross patterns up and down his backside, six to be exact. Each one cruel-looking to a novice eye. Blood bubbles to the surface, hovering just beneath the skin. In traditional play with paddles, floggers, canes, and whips, you start off slow to build your sub's tolerance. The deep-rooted masochist inside Tyler needs way more than that. He craves the immediate agony. The sweet relief that excruciating pain can bring him. We never follow typical constructs in our sessions. Edge-play, not to be confused with edging, doesn't follow those guidelines. It teeters on the edge of insanity and enlightenment. Bullwhips aren't for the faint of heart or those without proper training. I worked three years as a dungeon house Mistress, four days a week, before I opened my own practice. I was taught by some of the best Doms in the world on how to wield the tools of my trade. In simple terms, this isn't for beginners, ladies and gents. You're not a cowgirl, don't act like one.

Allowing Tyler's pain to smolder, I return to my wall of toys and exchange the bullwhip for a hefty flogger. Then I move down to my special area. Tapping my chin, humming to myself, I contemplate which colorful plug I should use on him tonight. My assistant sets Tyler's personal plugs and dildos on the display shelves before our sessions. She does the same with the rest of my clientele in their respective rooms. I don't like toys to be hidden away. Seeing what might be used on you can be fun—a tease. The five to pick from vary in style, size, and shape. From your standard beginner's taper that's barely more than a finger tickling your inner walls. To a thick anal-beaded progression. A hallow-cored mid-grade dilator that can be a lot of fun if you want to use a vibe at the same time. Or, my personal favorite, the ultimate prostate milker: it's curved, solid stainless steel, four inches at its widest, and rocks Tyler's world. Because I can, I pluck it off the shelf and return to my writhing man, whose chorus of moans make me wanna ride his dick until we're both spent. In due time.

Tossing the flogger to the floor, I approach my masochist, spread his cheeks, and without further ado, insert the head of the massager up his rectum. Tyler's sweat-soaked head falls back, a choked moan rattles in his throat through the resistant slide. He presses his ass out, knowing what toy this is, wanting it all. I give him another inch, and his restraints begin to rattle. Another nudge and Tyler's wailing. To heighten his arousal, I drag a nail across one of his slash marks. The decibel of his raspy cry echoes off the walls, body flailing beautifully. It's a good thing my cross is bolted down, or he'd come crashing to the floor.

I press in further until I'm halfway inside his slick passage.

"Mistress!" Tyler sings, breaking our unspoken rule of no language when in session. But he can't fully sign. Not tied like this. I'll forgive his indiscretion this once. It's not like he can help it.

To test where Tyler's flying inside that brilliant mind of his, I triple tap his hip—our universal sign to tell me what color he's at.

"*G,*" he forms with his shaky right hand, indicating green.

Perfect. We're halfway there.

I draw another nail down an angry, red mark, and insert the steel another inch.

Sweat cascades down Tyler's flushed cheeks, his chest rising and falling through laden breaths.

Smiling wickedly, I fuck into his hole, implanting to the hilt, then twist the base to settle it on his prostate. Tyler groans, thighs quaking under the strain of pleasure. If he's not careful, this toy will make him come. He's far too gone already, but he knows better than that. To reward him for his control, I slip a finger between the seam of my crotchless panties and into the wetness that conjures there. Swirling my fingertip around my entrance, I bite back a moan that he can't hear anyhow. *Damn,* I wanna come. I wanna come so hard. Why does Tyler have to be so perfect? Oh, the naughty, depraved things I want to do to him. Fuck him, spank him, turn him into a quivering mess at my feet. To make him lick me until I explode all over his cunt sucking lips.

Shit.

I need to chill before I lose it.

To calm my lecherous inner beast, I rest my forehead on Tyler's damp shoulder to balance my breathing. It does little to fix the sordid details flashing through my mind of him splayed before me, begging for touch, for my marks. I squeeze my thighs together, trapping my hand in the growing wetness. His masculine scent invades my nostrils, his fragmented moans shooting straight to my groin. My gums ache to make him feel me for days.

Ejecting a frustrated breath, I throw caution to the wind and sink my teeth into sweet flesh. Tyler moans. I moan louder, tasting the salt brine of him beneath my tongue. Damn him. Damn temptation. Damn lack of control! In for a penny, in for a pound, I widen my stance and finger my pussy because it's impossible not to. I need him too much.

On delicious repeat, I drive a single digit in and out of my slick walls, tormenting my achy g-spot, bringing myself higher and higher until the brink of no return is imminent. Sweat beads on my brow. Breasts rise and fall with the urge to climax. Thighs tense. Toes flex. But I can't come. Not yet. I don't deserve it any more than he does.

Expelling a sigh of regret, I yank my hand away, unlatch my teeth, step to the side like a poised Mistress who isn't about to lose her composure and lift my well-used finger to Tyler's parted lips. Because he's a good sub who deserves better from me, I paint my essence across the cupid's bow and puffy bottom lip. His tongue flicks out, tasting me there. I watch his eyelids flutter their appreciation as a pool of pre-cum grows on the floor between his thighs, thanks to the leash pointing his crown there.

I kiss the cap of his shoulder.

Tyler looks at me out of the corner of his eye, the small curve at the edge of his lips is a most welcomed, *hello, thank you,* and *I love you,* all at once.

"I love you, too," I mouth in return, also breaking the unspoken rule. Who cares anymore, I've already pleasured myself when I shouldn't have. Perhaps I could control these urges of mine if we'd play more. Twice a week is barely a flicker of what any of us needs. Maybe *more* is the answer. More sex. More time. More marks. More love. A gluttony of *more* to satiate this between us... the three of us.

I drop a lingering kiss to the same spot, making eye contact with my lover for a long, intense moment before I snap the connection and do what needs to be done.

Three taps on his hip to confirm.

"*G,*" he signs.

It's time to bring my man to gold.

Picking the flogger off the floor, I widen my stance, grip the leather handle not too hard, yet not too soft, and deliver a few practice swings into the air. The leather falls glide beautifully, just as I want. I'll definitely be sore tomorrow after wielding this. You'd think as much experience as I have, I'd be accustomed to the weight. But it doesn't work that way. I only bring out the big guns, aka my bison flogger, when I want Tyler to crest silver or gold. The smaller, easier-to-exercise floggers are used for tamer sessions. We're not going for the slap tonight, we're going for the punch.

After I get a good feel for its guided movements, I coil my strength and meet leather to flesh. The *thud* resonates, a wail of ecstasy follows, weaving together like a golden spun melody. Again, I whip Tyler's back in precise placement. He lifts onto the balls of his feet, resting his forehead on the pad I installed for moments like this. I unleash a third strike, a fourth, fifth, sixth, and his cries of pure bliss taper off as bright red heat blooms across his toned back. By the tenth, his body begins to sag, and my muscles burn from exertion—a sign that we're getting where he needs me to take him. By the fifteenth, Tyler's body goes slack, resting entirely on the slight incline of the cross. His shoulders lift and fall from heavy respirations. Sweat gleams across his entire frame.

Giving my poor arm a reprieve, I triple tap Tyler's hip and watch closely at his right hand that forms into a *P* for purple.

Two colors to go.

We're almost there.

The flogger has done its duty.

Kicking my heels to the side because I can't take them anymore, I toss the flogger on top of them to deal with later. It's time to be with my floaty sub, to break him in the name of art. Kneeling behind Tyler, I massage his calves that have not been touched, before I unlatch him from the cross and slide his legs together. To get my fill, I rub his thighs and ass as well. Both have been left unscathed, compared to his gloriously marred back.

Prying his cheeks apart, still resting on my haunches, I lick around the plug, waking up the nerve endings there. Tyler shivers. I call that a victory, considering his state of mind, so I play with him a little more. Paying special attention to his taint that needs kisses, too. By the time I pull away, my tongue is cramping, and he's soaked in saliva.

I grab onto Tyler's hips to help myself up. It's time to bring him over to the bed. Massaging up his biceps and forearms, loosening them as I go, I unhook his wrists from the shackles, setting him free. Still not moving from his spot, Tyler's head tips to the side, his cheek smashed to the cushion on the cross. Dazed eyes search for mine. I cup his sweaty cheek.

"Come with me. To the bed," I speak aloud, knowing he can read lips.

Tyler nods once and pries himself off the cross. He's wobbly getting to his feet at first. Not wanting him to lose his balance, I hook my arm around his waist and escort my sub to the bed, where I bend him over the edge. He goes without protest. Folding in half, his ass high in the air, leash half coiled on the floor, upper body supported by the mattress, I separate his legs how I want them and test their strength by pushing down on his hips. They resist buckling so I know we're good to go for what I have planned next.

This is going to be fun.

Skipping to the toy wall, excited, a smile playing on my face, I grab a cane, my favorite lube off the shelf next to the plugs, and my strap-on with pink cock attachment. Tyler's going to need this dick all night long to keep him in the zone. Nothing says I love you like your Mistress's ding-a-ling up your behind. If he's good, I'll let him put his inside me, too. Maybe. Probably. Okay, yes. I'll let him. I desire his pierced thickness as much as he desires my fake rubber one.

Necessities in hand, I return to the bed and set the cane on the sheets beside my masochist. It's time to gear up before we get started. Stepping into the black harness, I insert my dildo through the hole and adjust the straps for a snug fit around my waist. Because I love my dick so much, I pump it a few times for good measure. Men do it, so why can't I? It's fun. I highly advise all of my lady friends to wear a penis at least once in their life, to understand what it's like. There's something powerful about it. Instinctual. Base. Desirable. It's one of the best sex toys to experience, in my humble opinion. Sure, you don't get the direct pleasure, but the mental arousal it evokes is akin to climax without the explosive release. It's a gentler one. One that hums beneath the surface for hours, getting you wet, making you squirm as you watch your partner lose themselves under you, because of you, for you.

Ready, I retrieve my cane and reach between Tyler's legs to give him a languid pump that makes him shiver. A dribble of pre-cum wets my palm. I use it to lube my own dick before taking a step back. Just as I did with the flogger, I practice aiming the cane. This isn't the thick piece of wood your grandma uses to hobble around. We're talking a thin rattan stick that's going to bruise and stripe my lover's ass. It's one of his favorite toys. As are any of them that leave lasting impressions.

Adjusting my posture, I raise my arm and in one fluid motion, *whoosh* through the air, land the cane flush across both cheeks, branding them *mine*. On impact, Tyler clenches the sheets in his fists and moans broken and desperate for release. I deliver the next slash of pain, and his knees almost buckle. Tear-stained eyes, begging to let him climax stare back at me from the mattress.

I shake my head.

He ousts a rickety breath, offering an infinitesimal nod of submission.

I unleash another stripe.

His knuckles turn to snow.

Tears leak onto the sheets.

His nose reddens.

Tyler bites his bottom lip, shuddering through the blistering pain and the plug that intensifies the ecstasy that rages there.

Knowing exactly what he needs, I set free a torrent of pleasure-laced agony on his bottom one mighty blow after the next. Ten full seconds pause between strikes, giving him time to absorb the sharp sensation he craves. By ten his eyes no longer focus. At twenty, his face goes slack, lips parted. Thirty, fingers lose grip on the silk as his knees turn into overcooked noodles. By the time we crest fifty, our max during any scene, the bed is the only thing left supporting his body. His legs have officially failed. Deep bruising has already set in on his butt, and his breathing is oddly serene—the ultimate high. The intense ache in my shoulder means nothing compared to my wrecked sub, lost to his own mind. I relish in it. Smile, even.

This is what it means to experience real love. Real trust. To allow *your person* to shatter your walls until you're a puddle of nothingness, right where you need to be.

Stepping behind my lover, tossing the cane to the floor, I trace my fingers down the contours of his back. That's right. I did that. I created those marks... all of them. They're beautiful. So beautiful. Tyler barely moves beneath my touch. To some, this would be worrisome. To me, it's victory. It means that Tyler is swimming in heaven, the safe space inside his head that only he can visit. The place he vacations to draw inspiration from. Where the world outside doesn't exist, where he can be himself.

I tap his hip and wait.

Nothing.

I tap again, three times.

"S," he forms... barely.

Silver.

We're there.

On the cusp.

I can taste it.

Reaching between his cheeks, I remove the plug from his bottom and toss it onto the bed. Holding Tyler's glutes apart, I watch his dilated hole open and close in search of my love, tempting me to take it. If that's what he wants, who am I to deny him? Snatching the bottle off the sheets, I lube myself up and drive home, where I belong, inside Tyler. Hips meeting ass, he comes to, his toes finding purchase on the floor to keep him afloat. Drawing a knee up, Tyler crawls onto the bed. I follow suit until I'm left straddling his thighs with my dick buried to the hilt.

If only I could feel his heat surrounding it, hugging it, loving it as much as he loves me. It's moments like this that I wish my cock was real. Not because I want the pleasure it would bring, but the additional connection I would have with Tyler because of it.

To further our intimacy, I flatten my breasts to his back as my pelvis cradles him. Our fingers interlace above his head, and I draw back. Knowing what Tyler needs next, I bite into the base of his neck at the same moment I fuck his hole. A lethargic moan slips free from my sub. Again, I saw in and out, using our interwoven fingers and hips to propel me, to dig deep, 'cause that's what's necessary to achieve gold. For him, I must own his body, mind, and soul for this to work. If it was easy, anyone could do it. But it's not. A masochist of his caliber is rare, a needle in a million haystacks. And he's mine to keep.

My heart batters my breastbone at our closeness. The radiant warmth of Tyler's back soaks into my front. The thrum of his pulse beats alongside mine. I pepper kisses across the base of his neck, his shoulders and into his hairline. Sweat coats my lips like a balm that I crave more of. Broken noises emit from the deepest recesses of his soul, and tiny tremors wrack his frame. Needing to see more, to feel more, I pull away and flip my lover onto his back. Without any help, I shove his legs up, move the leash to the side, and re-enter his tunnel in one smooth glide, bottoming out.

Tyler reaches out for me, dazed, wanting me in his arms, needing me there. I comply because I want nothing more than to do just that. Thrusting in short jabs, drawing my pleasure from his, Tyler's dick folds between us as his legs wrap around my waist. I curve my arms under his shoulders, using them for leverage. Intense heat seeps into my palms there. Lining up, our noses brush, pecs smash to breasts, cleavage spilling over the top of my outfit. Hot puffs of air burst across my lips. I trace my tongue over his cupid's bow wanting to express how much I love him. Tyler answers my inner yearning with a kiss of his own. It's slow and sweet as we meld together, bringing tears to my eyes. Unadulterated happiness blooms in my heart.

This is as close as we can get or gold will fade, and nothing will be accomplished.

Knowing what needs to be done, I reluctantly pull out of our embrace to sit back on my feet. It's time.

"I love you," I sign, making eye contact before wrapping my fist around his erection that's slick with pre-cum, and give it four arousal-spiking pumps.

"I love you, more," Tyler replies, watching me, not his member.

"This is it."

"Yes," he agrees.

"No coming."

A nod.

"I mean it. Now place your hands behind your head and lift up your legs."

He complies. Knees toward his chest, hands threaded behind his neck.

"Keep them there."

A stiffer nod of obedience.

Taking the top quarter of the leash into an idle hand, I flatten my lover's dick to his stomach with the other and crash the thick, leather handle to his nuts.

There's no warm-up. No warning. It's swift and brutal. Tyler convulses, yet retains his position like a good sub. I do it again, harder and quicker than before, giving little reprieve. He sputters a string of nonsensical words. Three more in rapid succession and his eyes roll into his skull, feet shaking. His abs contract. Chest heaves for oxygen. Cock jumps up, flinging pre-cum, then resettles. To counteract the sensations, I slam my dick into his hole, draw back, and batter his nuts once again. Tyler moans, his voice hoarse, forehead scrunched in pleasurable pain. I fuck him more, swapping between owning his insides and bruising his precious jewels. If he wants gold. Oh, I'm gonna give him gold. He's gonna sing for me real soon. Sing to the heavens as he begs for me to let him come. But I won't. He doesn't get to climax. He gets to float in the world I drove him to, wearing my marks.

To gain better traction, I grip Tyler's hip with one hand, still wielding the leather in the other. Bracing my legs on the mattress, ready to bring my man home, I fuck him to the beat of Manson's *Sweet Dreams*—wreck him until he's left a quaking mess. And just when I think he might not be able to handle any more, I give it to him anyway because he needs it.

That's it.

Almost there.

Fat droplets of sweat pour down my face, muscles aching from overuse; yet, I power on, and drag my nails down his shaft, digging them in, on the cusp of drawing blood. Soaking up my love, Tyler's head tips back, neck elongating, as he sings for me a beautiful song of ecstasy.

"Missstresss! Missstresss! Misss..."

Tyler's eyes fly open, his blown pupils begging to come undone.

Shaking my head, I deny him.

Reveling in my refusal, a roar of gluttonous moans burst from Tyler's lips. His entire body trembles violently, dangling off the ledge, ready to jump.

Instead of giving in, I screw him harder, throw the leash to the side, and grip his balls. Then, locking eyes with my lover, I squeeze, and I squeeze until I see it... the moment his body submits to me, to the pain, to us, to *gold*. A calm washes through him amidst the hot and heavy. It's quite a sight. One I wouldn't believe if I didn't see it with my own eyes. Tyler's foundation has been cracked in two, and he's there, where he needs to be. His unfocused eyes see me, yet don't. No words are spoken as I pull out and climb off the bed.

"Come." I wave my sub forth, and he follows.

Curling into the seated position, Tyler's movements are slow and dreamlike. I don't have to ask where he's at to know. Gold's unique. Almost ethereal. Different than all the other colors he experiences.

Offering him my hand, Tyler slips a palm into mine, and I help him stand. He's very much a newborn colt at first. But after a few seconds, he's steady enough to be guided to his art corner, where a blank canvas and paints await.

Side by side we pause in his space, *being*, breathing. Tyler doesn't move to unleash his brilliance. He simply waits for my approval, refusing to break our roles. Like every other session where he creates, I'm the one who lifts his hand to the canvas, to lay it upon the middle.

"Paint me your heart," I sign.

"I will paint you everything."

Tyler's sweetness slams into me, right where it's most tender, as it always does. To show my appreciation, I press a simple kiss upon his lips.

"I will keep you on gold, wherever you need to be. Go on, show me what's inside."

He smiles softly, his handsome face lost in wonderment. "Thank you, Mistress. Love you."

"And I, you. Always."

"Always."

4

FRIENDSHIP & FUCKERY

Flipping over onto my stomach, face planted in the pillow, I groan, wishing I was dead. I need more sleep, a tub of aspirin, and a full-body massage to rival all massages. Last night wrecked me. Five hours after we reached gold, we continued to play in ecstasy-laden intervals. It was magical. Screwing Tyler on his knees, covered in speckles of paint, as he fought his climax. Ball crushing. Nails imbedding in his already ruined flesh, to sate his lust. The moans. Paddles. And erection that never waned. All in the name of art and love. In the name of *us*. For my Tyler.

To check if he skipped out already, I blindly pat his side of the bed. As predicted, he's gone. How he can walk today is beyond me. Sitting will be a bigger challenge. Hell, wearing a stitch of clothing will have him wincing in pain. A feeling he, no doubt, delights in. One I'm sure has him rock solid at this very moment.

"Don't pretend you're still asleep, bitch, I can hear you groan," Kendra, my assistant, singsongs—the whore.

I tilt my head to the side, cheek smooshed to the pillow. "Fuck you. You didn't just run a sadomasochism triathlon."

A pleased chuckle echoes through the space. *Bitch.*

Is it bad I can't even open my eyes? I'm bone tired. It was totally worth it, though. Every single second of it.

"When did he leave?" I adjust my leg and think better of it. Painkillers first, movement later. Mid-thirties sucks.

"He texted at seven."

Dang, that's early. Tyler's a morning person. One of those cheery, wide-awake people that everyone pretends to hate while secretly wishing they were like them. Besides me. I loathe mornings and alarm clocks with a passion.

"You do realize it's weird that my submissive texts you," I tease. It would be odd if I wasn't used to it. After two years, it becomes the norm.

Kendra, not having any of my sass, *tsks* good-naturedly. "He wanted to inform me that he'd left, so I could come in. You know you'd have a goddamn conniption if I came to clean and found your precious Tyler naked in bed. He also made me promise I'd call Raoul today for a ninety-minute massage. Reschedule your overly physical clients for the next three days. Order lunch from that Italian restaurant you love. Let his assistant in when she came by to shoot photos, take care of you without complaining too much, and," she sighs as if exhausted by the list, "arrange the flowers he sent, so his *a-ffec-tion* would be spread throughout the house. His exact words. Honestly, I gagged a little at that. Nobody besides Tyler talks that way."

As Kendra prattles on and on, the warm and fuzzies grow in the pit of my stomach until I'm about to burst. I can't believe he did that. Not that I should be surprised. For being a submissive, he's the one who cares for me outside of the bedroom. Maybe not sexually, but in all the ways that truly count. Whatever I did to deserve him, I'll never know. Nor will you hear me complain.

"More flowers?" I test to make sure I heard her correctly.

"Roses this time. Hot pink. One red."

"How many?"

"Ten dozen, maybe more."

"*Jeeesus,*" I hiss, curling my hands underneath me, grimacing through the pain. If I don't move, I'm right as rain. I'm not a fool, there will be no more moving for me.

"Yep. That man sure knows how to declare his intentions."

No kidding.

"And what about his assistant?" Kali's a cool, emo chick, who's always respected me. I can see why Tyler keeps her around. She's efficient and appreciates his art without being a crazed fan who wants to have his babies. Yes, famous painters have groupies, too. Especially sexy ones like Tyler. He's my very own version of a Shawn Mendes, Justin Bieber mashup. Super gorgeous. Super talented. Extra amazing. If you think for one second that his deafness is a turn-off for women, you'd be dead wrong. If anything, it makes him more intriguing, more desirable. Kali had to start running his Instagram last year when the fans became too much to handle. Shirtless painting photos are quite the aphrodisiac for some.

"You know." Kendra moves about the room, doing what, I dunno.

"He didn't."

He'd better not have. Not this time. We agreed he'd stop doing it.

"He did. If your sexy ass turned over, you'd see the letter he left for you on his pillow like some cheesy heartthrob in a cliché romantic comedy."

I don't move.

It's too difficult.

I promise I'm not normally this much of a whiny baby.

"Way to kill it for me, Kendra. Way to... Kill. It. You can leave now." I give her hell. What kind of boss would I be if I didn't? She has to earn her keep. Dildo washing and all.

"Not until you get up. You have two clients today. Per Hottie McMasochist's orders, I've lightened your workload for the next three days. Moved Gary and Leo to today. Bonez and Jerry are tomorrow before Rob gets off work. I also texted Rob to confirm."

Why does she meddle so much when I'm perfectly capable of handling my own relationships? Unless...

"Tyler told you to do that, too, didn't he?"

"Yes. He also left his credit card on the counter in the kitchen."

Of course, he did. Silly, silly, sweet man.

"I'm not using that."

"I already did, to order your lunch. It'll be delivered in an hour."

I groan, bested.

Kendra isn't supposed to encourage this. She's supposed to be on my side. The side that doesn't let Tyler take care of me. The side that keeps him from winning this year-long debate about where our relationship is going. For being in his twenties, almost a full ten years younger than me, you'd think I would be the one looking to settle down. Ya know, with my biological clock ticking and whatnot. Not that he'd be the one pursuing more—my ever-demanding romantic.

"When's Raoul coming?" I change the subject, not wanting to argue that she could've used my credit card that she has access to 24/7.

"After your first appointment. That's the soonest he could squeeze you in."

"You didn't tell Tyler, did you?" I hope not.

"That I couldn't get you a massage before your first client? *Pft*. No. I don't have a death wish, Ronan."

"*He* wouldn't kill you."

"No. But he'd tell Rob, which is pretty much the exact same thing."

This is true. Rob's intense. He and Kendra have quite the love-hate relationship. More hate than love. She thinks he's an intolerable, misogynistic bastard. While he thinks she's an idiot. In Kendra's defense, Rob does come across as a misogynistic bastard to most people. In reality, he's misunderstood.

"Your secret's safe with me," I vow.

Kendra claps her hands twice, too enthusiastic for my taste. "Thank you. Now, up! Your threesome with coffee, Motrin, and Tylenol is waiting. Then you gotta shower. It smells like sex in here."

I grin like the deviant I am. "That's because we had sex. Lots and lots of hot, hot, ho-*t* kinky sex."

We did. Loads of yummy penetration. The deep, soul-tethering kind. I fucked him on the floor, on the bed, bent over the chair arm. When we were both exhausted beyond rationale, Tyler escorted me back to the bed, where he entered me, stretched my walls with his studded girth, pumped twice, and came in a rush. Like a strike to my match, I set off alongside him, moaning his name, lips molded together. Wrung the heck out from our session and subsequent orgasms, we promptly passed out in a tangle of sweaty limbs and whispers of sweet nothings. It was ah-mazing.

"I'm sure you did. But you don't need any of Tyler's tadpoles getting loose during your session with Gary."

"Remind me again why I—"

"Because you love me, can't live without me, and need me to clean up this godawful mess. Jesus, Ronan, how many times did you let the boy come?" The irritated *tap tap tap* of her toe resounds.

I roll my otherwise closed eyes. It might not count as much, but I can still feel them tip into my skull. Someone's a tad overdramatic today, considering what she cleans on an almost daily basis.

"That's *lube*. Not cum. You know me better than that." It wasn't intentional. Down came the hot subby, to the ground. The bottle went *boom*. My cock went *weeee* up a slippery chute. We moaned. Then humped like jackrabbits. Case closed.

"Oh. Well. That's better. I thought you were losing your touch."

As if.

"I have way more control than that."

"Touché, Mistress Bossy Butt. Now up, up!" The comforter is torn off the bed, leaving me stark naked.

I open my eyes for the first time and glare at the

devil. If the devil was a slender, plum breasted, red-haired, feisty goddess from the underworld, who wears shorty shorts and ballet flats in lieu of flip-flops because she hates feet, including her own.

"You're fired," I grumble.

The whore smiles, flashing her pearly whites. "See, you did have a great night."

"I hurt, *everywhere*."

The toffee-eyed broad rolls those bad boys with dramatic flair, hand hooked on her hip. My blanket lies in a heap at her feet. "Boo. Hoo. Hoo. Poor Mistress Ronan got to screw her sexy submissive all night long." She snorts at her sarcasm and flicks a finger toward the nightstand where my pills and a steaming cup of coffee rest.

Taking a deep breath, I force myself into a seated position, legs dangling over the edge of the mattress. I swipe up the pills, toss them into the back of my throat, palm the mug, and take a swig to assist the painkillers down. Perfect temperature. Even better taste.

Shoulders hunching, I sigh, taking another drink that warms my core.

Coffee is life.

I take mine with two sugars and a large splash of flavored creamer. It's late summer time, so I go with my usual caramel or French vanilla. In winter, I'm a festive one. The basic bitch in me comes out to play when the pumpkin spice does. That stuff is like crack dressed in a colorful bottle.

Kendra, knowing I won't lie back down once I'm up, starts cleaning while I snatch the neatly folded letter off Tyler's pillow and open it.

To my gorgeous Mistress,

Thank you for one of the best nights of my life. I promise to make up for my portion of sex the next time we see each other. I'm embarrassed I didn't last longer. I also need to taste your pussy during our next session as well. Make a mental note of that. Because you deserve nothing more than to come repeatedly on my face. Getting tongue cramps while pleasuring you would be an honor.

On the easel is your latest gift. I know you'll argue that you can't keep it like you always do. Please don't. I love sharing my talent with the woman I love. By now Kendra should have told you about Kali stopping by to snap pictures for us to make prints to sell. After that, please hang it somewhere in the main house. Wherever you think it fits best is fine with me.

Can't wait to see you on Monday at our dinner with Rob. Sorry I skipped out early. I have tons of colorful images flowing through my head today, thanks to you, and didn't want the inspiration to go to waste.

Text later if you're up for it.

Don't overdo it. I know how sore you get after our all-nighters.

Love you always,
Ty

P.S. Don't scold me about the flowers. You can spank me for them later. You know we both want that.

P.S.S. I'm sore as fuck, too. It'll be a miracle if my boner goes down in the next week.

P.S.S.S. Miss you already and I haven't even left

yet.
P.S.S.S.S. You're beautiful when you sleep.

Swallowing the emotional knot in my throat, heart fluttering, I set the letter on the nightstand to keep, finish my coffee, and force myself to stand. It's dull and achy at first. Thankfully, as I shuffle my feet closer to the painting, the stiffness uncoils.

Naked as the day I was born, I stand in front of Tyler's latest creation and gasp. A single tear treks down my cheek. I chew my bottom lip, soaking in the delicate brushstrokes. I tuck an arm across my chest, cradling my opposite elbow.

Kendra sidles up behind me, tucking the long strands of my hair over my shoulder. My braid fell out at some point last night. "He painted you again," she whispers, raking through my curls with her fingers.

I bob my head, refusing to fall to pieces, not today, not now. Art is meant to evoke emotion. Tyler's art goes beyond that. It changes a person. It changes me.

"I love how he placed you in the smoke, rising from the fire like a deity the goblins are worshiping."

She's right. That's what he did. It's a night scene set inside the forest. In the center of the painting is a roaring fire. Dancing around it are little creatures. Some are chubby, lifelike goblins, the others are winged nymphs that sparkle. They're all naked, as is the goddess rising from the smoke, billowing into the sky. The likeness of the woman is uncanny. From the shape of my hips, and the curve of my belly, to the feminine grace of my shoulders, all are displayed in the utmost accuracy. As the smoke dissipates, the stars form and a blood moon casts its eerie glow on the creatures below.

Lost in the scene, Kendra and I stand together for however long, appreciating Tyler's talent.

"I love how the trees and the smoke look like they're blowing in the wind," I mutter to myself.

"The pixie creatures are all women," Kendra remarks.

They are.

"Their boobs look lifelike." Perky. Rosy tipped. Firm.

"Look at that white-haired one. She's the only one wearing a crown of flowers."

"Maybe she's the queen." I shrug one shoulder.

"She might be."

I point to a green goblin without touching the canvas. "Look at him. He's erect."

"He's staring at the woman in the smoke. You think that's Tyler and he's watching you?"

Looking a little closer, I gasp, covering my mouth. "It is. Look at his back, Kendra. Oh. My. God."

She leans in, her breasts pressing against my back. "Are those lash marks?"

"Yes. Those marks are just like the ones I give him."

"That's Tyler then." Kendra points to a big goblin standing beside a nymph, not far from Tyler. "Is that Rob, you think?"

"Possibly. He does have half an erection. The rest of the goblins are limp."

"He's also staring at you, the rest of the goblins aren't... He does this a lot, you know. Painting you, himself, and Rob. You do know what's going to happen come Monday." Kendra wraps her arm around my waist from behind, hand splaying below my belly button as she nuzzles her nose to the space beneath my ear. I should've known she would take this opportunity to cop a feel. I suppose this is when I tell you that Kendra's bisexual... and I've always been bi-curious. She's the only woman I've ever experimented with. It doesn't happen often, but it does happen. Rob and Tyler are well aware of this and have never cared. It was something all four of us sat down together and discussed two years ago when things got serious with Tyler, Rob, and me. Kendra understands that we are friends, first and foremost, employee and employer second, and sexual partners last. Sure, there's love on both our parts. It's just not the kind of love you feel for a life partner. It's the one you feel for a friend that you find attractive.

"Is someone wanting a little something?" I tease, rubbing my ass against her crotch.

Kendra's breath kicks up in my ear as she glides her hand to my pussy where she splits my cleft with a finger to rub my clit. I gasp a breathless moan on contact, head falling back to rest on her shoulder, giving her a clear invitation to play.

"Did Tyler tell you to do this, too?" I rasp.

Her teeth nip my earlobe. "You're naked, Ronan, you know how wet that makes me."

"It does, does it?"

To punctuate her desire, Kendra adds a second finger and my legs begin to shake, my orgasm too close for comfort. *Damn.* She's good at this. Too good.

Taking the upper hand, I grab Kendra's dainty

wrist and remove her from my sex. She chuckles in my ear. "Mistress Ronan is afraid to come, isn't she?"

"Shut up, slut." Whipping around, hair flying, I draw my Domme to the surface, palm both of Kendra's shoulders, and push her to her knees. She moans all the way to the floor, her eyes hooded with unspent lust.

Reaching for me, she licks her lips, greedy for a taste. I slap her hands away. "Tell me."

"I asked them," she husks, her chest rising and falling in rapid succession.

"Asked who, what?"

"Rob and Ty. I asked if I could make you come today."

"I thought my lunch would be here soon."

"I ordered it an hour out so we could play first."

"I haven't showered."

"I know."

"I'll taste of Tyler."

Kendra groans, her eyes sliding shut as if that's the sexiest thing she's ever heard. "Yesss," she hisses through her teeth.

Satisfied with Kendra's reply, I cup the back of her head, widen my stance, and feed her my cunt.

Without pause, my favorite rug muncher goes to town on my clit, sucking it into her mouth. Flicking it wildly with her tongue, she slides two fingers inside my pussy. I grip a fistful of her red hair for balance.

"That's it," I groan. "Eat me."

In response, Kendra sucks harder, her fingers plunging in and out of my wetness at a possessed pace. A shiver races through me, starting at my toes, ending in my fingertips. That's it. *Fuck. Yes!* I'm gonna come all over her gorgeous face. My clit throbs on the edge. I grind against her lips, slathering them in my juices. She moans for more, and I give it to her with pleasure.

"Finger yourself," I demand, wanting her to get something out of this, too. She's not like Tyler; she doesn't get off on denial.

The stubborn broad shakes her head.

"Finger yourself, slut."

Another defiant shake.

Kendra's not a sub, so she doesn't get off on obedience. She's quite the opposite. The firecracker likes to be difficult.

Wrenching her face from my cunt using her hair, I take a step back.

Glistening eyes and swollen lips coated in me, stare up, begging me to let her keep going. I don't, because I hate disobedience.

"Take off your shorts." I nod toward said garments, and she works fast at removing them, knowing I don't play games.

I praise her by relaxing the punishing hold on her hair without letting go.

"Spread your knees."

She does, giving me a sexy-as-hell view of her curly red thatch and smooth, dewy slit. I lick my own lips at the sight. Before Kendra, I never tasted anyone's pussy but my own. Never had the desire to. Until one day she asked if she could touch me. Just like that. No hesitation. We'd been working together for over a year at that point, I knew she was bisexual, so I wasn't upset. I was intrigued. The first time I ate her was equal parts scary and arousing. Now all I wanna do is lick her tangy sweetness until she begs me to stop. That's the bonus of being with a woman, they can come nonstop if you know what you're doing. Men can never feed your ego that way. Not like Kendra can.

"Two fingers. Inside. Now."

Chewing the inside of her cheek, Kendra shakes her head like a damn brat.

Fine.

She doesn't wanna listen.

I'll do it.

Shoving her shoulder, Kendra falls back, landing hard on her elbows, legs slipping out from under her. I drop to the floor in record time, and jam three fingers into her sopping wet cunt. Surprised by my reaction, Kendra tries to crawl away, but I don't let her. I fuck her slick tightness without remorse. Hard and fast, almost brutal, until she's writhing like a fish out of water, screaming incoherently.

That's what happens when you don't listen.

I take what I want.

And I want her to come all over me.

My opposite thumb joins in on the party to play with her fat clit that's peeking out from underneath its hood. It's a pretty little guy. One that makes my mouth water to taste.

"Ronan!" Kendra's walls squeeze around my fingers in a vise as she blows apart at the seams. Her head kinks back, neck elongates, chest heaving upward through a violent orgasm. Because I love her tiny tits, I rip her tank top down along with the cups of her bra to see her dusky pink areolas and matching nips. Thankfully she doesn't fight me on it. Rolling into a second climax will do that to ya.

I grin wide at her blissed-out expression but don't stop my fun.

Two soon turns into three, and when it does, I lean over my assistant and suck a ripe nipple into my mouth.

"Ronan. Oh. God. What are you—" To shut her up, I nibble the peak until it's as hard as a rock. This has her crashing again, blindly clawing at my shoulders. If this was planned, and my muscles didn't already ache, I'd fuck her with a strap-on. We've only done that once before. She loved it, as did I.

By the time I've brought my naughty slut to her sixth mind-blowing orgasm, I crawl over her face and sit 69 style to feast on each other. Pulling her legs up, knees bent, I dive face-first into her soaking center and lap up all the juices there. As soon as her tang awakens my taste buds, I'm a goner. I eat her like a madwoman. Loving every second of it, I groan smearing my face in it. I suck her clit, probe her entrance, and lap her crinkly backdoor because it deserves loving, too.

Palming my ass, moaning into my pussy, Kendra takes a tentative taste of my slit. I freeze my ministrations on her clitty. Her hot breath bathes my sex in heavy exhales. Sitting back, resting on her face, I grant her full access.

"Go on, make me come," I invite.

Heeding my words, Kendra doesn't disappoint as she goes to town on my cunt, eating, fingering, sucking—drawing pleasure from my center that blooms outward in a rush of ecstasy. I cry out her name, palming my tits, as I begin to ride her face, and she lets me. Welcomes it, even. There's no use in resistance when this is what we both want, so I give in full bore.

"Can you taste him?" I husk as she delves that sweet, sweet tongue into my sex.

Kendra hums in response.

"I wanna fuck you so badly." Closing my eyes, I fall deeper into the moment, directly in front of Tyler's painting.

This is incredible.

Suddenly, without warning, Kendra rolls me to the side, and I catch myself on the way down. Before I know what the hell is going on, she's scissoring our legs together, wet pussy grinding to wet pussy. Her plum tits bounce. Face screwed up in pleasure. She palms my breast, and that's all it takes. I'm coming. Hard. So fucking hard! Grabbing her arm to tether our connection, eyes slamming shut, back arching, I wail my release. Kendra doesn't relent. She rubs our cunts together faster, forcing my orgasm to flow forth. It doesn't stop. Everything tightens. My mouth falls open in delirious cries, yet she continues. Another crash of pelvises and she breaks apart again. I'm right behind her, acutely aware of how intense everything feels. To have her clit graze mine. Her fingers pluck at my nipple. Our folds kiss in a wet, slapping symphony. It lasts forever. Until neither of us can catch our breaths. Until I need her mouth on mine. So I draw her down to kiss in a tangle of sloppy tongues and hungry groans.

Lying on top of me, Kendra shoves two fingers into my entrance. I wrap my legs around her waist, our bare breasts mashed together. "Kendra," I whimper, feeling her wiggle inside, hitting my g-spot.

"I wanna fuck you, too, sexy." She drops a peck on my damp upper lip, hair falling around her face like a fiery angel.

The doorbell rings.

"Fuck!" we bellow in unison.

That's what I get for having an extra speaker placed in the dungeon.

Kendra drops a final kiss to my mouth, then scrambles to her feet. "That's gotta be your lunch. Come up when you're ready, take a shower, and I'll have your food plated at the table when you're done."

I reach out for her as she struggles adorably to get dressed. She trips a few times trying to get her shorts on. I grin at her just-fucked hair. Yep, I did that. Gave her those puffy lips, too, that are still coated in my essence.

Her hand folds into mine probably thinking I want help up. Instead I yank her down. Expelling a cute yelp, Kendra falls on top of me. I turn us onto our sides, take her mouth in a searing kiss, push the hem of her shorts to the side, and finger her to another quick, body-thrashing orgasm. When I'm finished, I help her to her feet, spank her hot ass, and watch with a giant smile plastered across my face, as she stumbles from the room, sputtering nonsense about me driving her crazy, and how perfect my tits are.

What a fun morning. I'd love to wake up like that every day. Sex. Orgasms. Kissing. Yes, please. Sign me up. If you add Rob and Tyler into the mix, I'd definitely be on board. Ecstatic even.

Rubbing both palms down my face, loving the smell of Kendra on them, I oust a satisfied groan. To feel her a little longer, I squeeze my legs together and rejoice in the fiery tingle that resonates there. If we could've kept going, I might have been able to come another ten times. Possibly more. Kendra's one talented friend. Her future wife or husband is one lucky sonofabitch.

Another sigh.

That's enough about all her yumminess.

It's time to shower.

After lunch, I have my first client.

If I remember correctly he's my splosher, aka likes cakes, and pudding poured on him while he jacks off. To heighten his enjoyment, I call him names. His favorite being *Mommy's little whore,* or my personal favorite *Daddy's filthy butt pirate* when he fingers his asshole. Isn't my job absolute perfection? I can't wait to see what Kendra bought for his session today. I'm hoping for cheesecake. That's super fun to throw at a person. It leaves tiny red marks that don't last. And you know how much I enjoy marking people, even if it's temporary.

5

TEXTUAL ENCOUNTERS OF THE HOT KIND

Sitting on my sofa, feet propped on the leather upholstered ottoman that moonlights as a coffee table, wearing a pair of boy shorts and spaghetti strap tank, I flip Grey's Anatomy on, using my Fire Stick. Now, this is a nighttime drama that speaks my language. It's sexy and adrenaline spiking. Not to mention, I usually learn a thing or two.

As I'm sure you've deduced, yes, my day is finally through. I just finished taking another shower. That would make three for the day. The sploshing sesh with Gary was quite messy. Kendra didn't get cheesecake. It was chocolate cream pies, German chocolate cake, and dark chocolate pudding that I got to throw at, or pour on my client. He loved every second of it. I have to admit, it was pretty fun to watch him roll around in food, jacking off his average-sized pecker while I degraded him. I had Gary so horned up at one point he took three fingers to his ass. Now that was sort of hot for a mid-fifties overweight man that I'm not attracted to. I donned my typical Domme garb for the session: pleather pants, bustier, sexy high-heeled boots, and braided hair.

After Gary, I showered, then got a massage that lasted close to two hours. Unlike most massage therapists, Raoul will touch your delicate parts if you ask. I met him at a ProDomme event three or four years ago, since he specializes in happy endings. Not that I ever partake in those. I have no need. But, I do love my ass, boobs, and vagina massaged. Trust me, there's nothing better than a full-body rub that includes those extras. I hurt in places I didn't even know hurt until he dug those magical thumbs in. It was pure heaven.

Leo was last, and that boy is a freak in the best of ways. Diapers. Bottles. Total littles play or AB/DL—adult baby, diaper lover. He wets his nappies, gets spanked on his tushie, plays with baby toys, and will eventually find a full-time mommy who'll let him suckle her breasts. I don't offer that so he makes due with my limits. I rock him in a rocking chair, give him pacifiers, feed him, and change his bottom—all in the name of kink. He usually sports an erection the entire time. Even wants me to swat his hand away when he tries to tug on it like a small child would. It's not my cup of tea, but I am more than happy to accommodate Leo. Our sessions last longer than most, around three hours. That gives us enough time for everything, including a climax that he achieves by rolling toy cars up and down his penis as I pretend to change his diaper. He's a biweekly regular that's super sweet. I'd happily take on twenty men like Leo as a client. Trust me, I've had way worse.

Once he was done, I met Kendra upstairs to log the day's events and hug her goodbye. Then I took a two-minute shower to wash the scent of baby powder from my skin. Now I'm here watching TV after I ate leftover lunch for dinner. This is the time of day I feel most alone. Not that I mind peace and quiet. I enjoy it. Then again, the idea of cuddling up next to a warm body, watching TV in our underwear, sounds divine.

To combat the increasing loneliness, I text my lads in our group chat. It makes things easier, and they don't seem to mind.

Me: **Done for the day. About to watch some Grey's. How are you two?**

I click on my show as I await a reply. Rob's off work by now so unless he's asleep or getting some, he's the one who'll answer quicker. Tyler needs to be torn from his art to text. After last night, I'll be surprised if he replies at all. He's likely submerged in various paintings. It's a struggle to make him eat, let alone communicate when he's in the zone.

Ten minutes in, Meredith and Alex are having a heart-to-heart.

My phone vibrates in my lap.

Rob: **Good, babe. Just lyin' in bed. How was your day? Not too sore, I hope. Did Kendra give you a big O like she wanted?**

Smiling like a silly teenager, I snuggle further into the sofa, snatch the blanket off the back that Tyler bought me, and throw it over my legs to get comfier.

Me: **Way to get straight to the point.**

Rob: **That's how I roll. Don't play coy. Tell me.**

My nose wrinkles at his misplaced dominance. It may not sound like much, but I can practically hear the sharp crack of his tone from here. I don't have to ask to know that Rob got laid tonight. Some honey from his club spread her legs, per usual. Did I forget to mention that Rob's a biker? Well, he is. A Crimson Outlaw to be exact. Unfortunately, his dickishness comes out in full force when he's high on endorphins after a faceless nut. Where Tyler has no desire to screw other women because he gets all he needs with me. Rob, the broody, anger-repressed, emotionally stunted man I love, needs his dominant side sated too. The side that craves control, and emotionless hardcore fucking. The Neanderthal, caveman aspect of his outward personality. A façade he portrays for every person besides me, and sometimes Tyler. I don't feed into his bullshit, and know when he's wearing his well-suited mask. Five years with a person you begin to read between the carefully constructed lines. And I consider myself a Rob expert.

Refusing to let on that I'm aware of his current *just fucked* state, I whip out the Domme.

Me: **Tyler's busy painting. He doesn't care right now. And you know better than to cop an attitude with me, Big Man.**

Rob: **Fuck.**

Rob: **I dunno what to say, Mistress.**

Rob: **I drank tonight with Prez. Some punk at work today decided he wanted to run his smart mouth and get in my face. I roughed him up when he wouldn't back down. Put him in the infirmary. Needed to let off some steam after so I went to Nowhere.**

Nowhere is his club's bar.

Rob's guilt is starting to sneak in. I can feel it. This is normal for us. We have the most functional dysfunctional relationship. It's better that I let him pour his guts out before responding.

Rob: **Fuck. Okay. Okay. I'm sorry. I. Fuck. You know this is hard for me to say. But I... ya know. Tomorrow is gonna be a good day. I'm comin' by after work.**

Tyler: **Hey, Mistress, Big Rob. Give me a sec to catch up on the thread.**

I heave a sigh of relief that Tyler's on. That means he hasn't gone cross-eyed from painting all day, or died from dehydration.

Tyler: **What the fuck, Rob? Apologize better than that. Mistress, I'm sorry for Rob the Knob's behavior. We do want to know how your day went and if Kendra got you off. But you don't have to tell us. How's the pain? Mine is fucking amazing. I've been hard as stone all day. My ass is as purple as an eggplant. Back looks like a tiger clawed it. Damn. We need to do that more often. I finished three paintings today besides yours.**

Rob: **Don't be a dick, boy. I said I was sorry.**

Tyler: **Don't call me boy. We've talked about this.**

Rob: **You're two years older than my own son. You're still a boy in my eyes.**

Tyler: **You do know I make more money than you.**

Rob: **And I have a bigger dick.**

Tyler: **So? Mine's pierced. #Winner**

Rob: **I can hear.**

Tyler: **Wow. Bravo. Good one, Rob the Knob. Teasing the deaf man. Haven't heard** that one before. ::*eye roll emoji*:: #IStillMakeMoreMoneyThanYou

I roll my eyes, too. This is getting ridiculous. Funny, yet stupid. Now can you see why Kendra hates Rob? He can be intense if you don't know how to handle him. Tyler does. That's why I'm not interfering. Plus, this is the best kind of free entertainment.

Rob: **Is your ass really the color of an eggplant?**

Tyler: **Not gonna apologize for being an asshole once again?**

Rob: **It's part of my charm.**

Tyler: **What charm? Nobody likes an asshole.**

Rob: **Mistress does.**

Tyler: **No. I'm pretty sure she likes it when she can sneak beneath that protective shell. You're a big ole teddy bear at your squishy center.**

Rob: **Now you're talking like a girl. What are you, my therapist?**

Tyler: **Mistress, are you seeing this? I think Rob deserves the anal-destroyer plug tomorrow for his childish behavior. Your call, though, beautiful.**

I snicker.

God, I love these men.

Rob: **Suck-up. And no to the anal destroyer. I don't like to be fucked like a bitch, like you do.**

Tyler: **Riiiiggghhhttt. Let's add liar to your ever-growing list of traits.**

Rob: **I don't.**
Tyler: **Uh huh. Suuure, I'm the only one who likes Mistress's big pink cock up my ass. At least I'm man enough to admit it. You are either drunk tonight, Rob the Knob, or you banged some club whore and are feeling guilty about it.**

Bingo.

I adore this man so much.

Rob: **Shut it, boy.**
Tyler: **Yes, Daddy.**
Rob: **Fuck.**
Tyler: **#DeafManForTheWin**
Rob: **I can't believe I... your eggplant-colored ass.**
Tyler: **Awe. How sweet. I love you too.**
Rob: **That's not what I was gonna say.**
Tyler: **Yes, you were. Don't lie. It'll make your dick smaller.**
Rob: **LOL. You're such a pain. Seriously, is your ass the color of an eggplant?**
Tyler: *(image: taut, insanely wrecked butt cheeks)*

Yep. That is the hottest thing ever. I scissor my thighs together at the gorgeous sight, wanting to finger myself. I did that. All of it. Gorgeous.

Me: **Your ass is always so sexy. Seeing my marks on it turns me on.**
Rob: **Damn. That's a beautiful ass. Mistress worked you over good.**
Tyler: **I've wanted to jack off about three dozen times today. But I won't. I'll probably have a wet dream tonight. Wouldn't be the**

first time after a session.

I hope he does. That's sexy as hell. He always sends us a picture of the mess if he does. Sheets covered in goo because he sleeps in the buff.

Me: **Did you wear a plug today?**

Tyler: **Did you want me to?**

Me: **I always want you in a plug. Put a medium size in to sleep with tonight. In the morning go larger. I want a picture. And to answer your question, yes, Kendra and I had sex today.**

Rob: **Fuck. I'm hard again. Put the plug in, Tyler. Listen to Mistress.**

Me: **I like it when you're hard for me. Both of you.**

Rob: **I'm always hard for you.**

Tyler: *(image: legs up, cheeks spread with one hand, the jeweled tip of a plug staring back at us.)*

Rob: **Does it feel good, boy?**

Tyler: **I need to come. It's hitting my prostate. Mistress, this is pure torture.**

Smiling wickedly, I push the edge of my panties to the side and run the tip of my finger through my silky wetness. I'm not gonna come tonight, but I love the thought of being extra worked up alongside my men. Even if they're not here, we can share in this together.

Me: **No jacking off, Tyler. You know better. Rob, the same goes for you. Keep your hands off that dick.**

Rob: *(Image: the crown of cock poking out of the top of boxer briefs, glistening pre-cum.)*

Tyler: **#IStillMakeMoreMoneyThanYou**

Rob: **Shut it, boy.**

Tyler: **Sorry, you two, but I gotta shower. I'm covered in paint. Prints for your new painting will be up on my site tomorrow, Mistress. Thought you might want to know. I hate to cut this short, but talking to you both is messing with my head on both ends. Love you both.**

Rob: **Night. Lookin' forward to seeing the painting tomorrow. Listen to Mistress, no jacking off. Enjoy the plug. It looks good in you.**

Tyler: **Stop with the compliments, Big Rob, or you'll lose that asshole rep.**

Rob: **Fuck off.**

Tyler: **And he's back.**

Another smile pulls from my lips at their banter. They do love each other in their own way. They have a different kind of bond I've never seen before. Tyler takes Rob's assholish ways in stride, just as I do. That's why we work.

Me: **I'm gonna sign off, too. Be good. I'll see you tomorrow, Rob. Love you both. Always.**

Rob: **I... you. You know what. Later.**

Chest full of hope and love, I return my attention to the TV.

Rewinding Grey's, I get through the episode and one more before I turn in for the night. Tomorrow's going to be a short day. I'm looking forward to it. Seeing Rob again can't come soon enough. I miss the giant dickhead like crazy.

6

DEMONS & DOMINATION

Seated on my velvet throne in the corner of the dungeon bedroom, legs crossed, wearing a black lace teddy, I patiently await Rob's arrival. It should be soon. Unlike with Tyler, I'm always the first to enter and set up the scene before the Big Man's appointment. Due to his past, it's not healthy for him to wait on me. His mind has a tendency to overthink, to worry about what's going to take place. I learned that the hard way when we first met, and he up and left before I got to the room. You see, Rob, my super sexy, macho man has childhood driven issues with sex. You can thank his Bible-thumping bigot of a mother for that. From an early age, he was taught that the simple act of kissing or hugging someone you're not related to is a mortal sin. Considering those warped beliefs, can you imagine her views on sex and masturbation? They were cruel to the nth degree. Rob still has switch scars on his backside for getting caught taking part in pleasures of the flesh. In other words, he kissed a girl at school in the fourth grade and ended up mutilated for it. All of this coming from a woman who screwed his father out of wedlock. The same father who cheated on his mother shortly after he found out she was pregnant. This, I believe, is what set her on the path of misguided faith and man-hatred. Rob never even jacked off until he left home at eighteen to join the military. Why would he when his wet dreams were also punished? Self-preservation has its merits.

As a result of his upbringing, Rob harbors an abyss of repressed anger, and struggles to enjoy sex because his subconscious still believes it's a sin. The faceless-club-girl fucking is an odd coping mechanism. He does it to release the anger, to show he's in control, that he can do it. The guilt of his actions sets in afterward. Sick, ready-to-puke, all-consuming guilt. The kind you can't wash off. The kind that makes him even angrier at himself. You can blame his mother, the evil spawn of Satan, for all of it. He tries to cope. He does. Although, he blames himself for not being strong enough to slay the demons his mother birthed. Those same demons cost him two marriages and numerous other relationships, and prevented him from having sex in any position other than doggy style. Why? Because he couldn't look at the women he penetrated. Aside from me, he still can't.

Readjusting myself in the chair, I grin impishly at the extra-large dildo suction cupped to the floor in the middle of the room, underneath a spotlight. Tyler suggested the addition last night through text, and I like the idea. It'll test Rob's limits for sure. Ones we've navigated around from the very beginning.

Five years ago, when Rob came to me looking for a Domme, the cocky asshole demanded pain. Lots and lots of pain, thinking it would solve his afflictions, which I didn't know about at the time. I obliged him because I assumed he was honest during the initial interview, most submissives are. They know what they crave. That's why they seek a Domme in the first place. After three less-than-enthusiastic sessions of medium flogging, I learned real quickly that Rob was repressing some deep, ugly shit. That was the moment I made the conscious decision to truly help him tear down his outer walls, so he could heal from the inside out. Every session, even now, is emotionally exhausting. You should know, just so you're prepared, at first Rob fights me tooth and nail. It's that survival instinct kicking in. Fight, not flight. He can be belligerent and oftentimes scary when he wants to be.

Tucking my braid over my shoulder, the door opens and in thuds my hunk in his well-worn motorcycle boots, holey jeans, a plain black t-shirt that's stretched to the max across his bulging muscles, and a black bandana tied around his forehead. He winks at me like the flirt he is and swipes the bandana off his forehead. It's the first thing to hit the floor. The rest will soon come.

He kicks the door shut with the heel of his boot, takes three steps closer, and pauses when he notices the blue dildo waiting for him.

"Fuck!" He retreats a step, his iron-forged walls bracing for impact.

Rob's thick fists flex down at his sides. Scruffy jaw clenches. Nostrils flare.

Expelling a heavy breath, he scrubs a palm over his short mohawk. I know it's a bit strange that both my men have mohawks. Tyler's is a messier faux hawk, whereas Rob's is clipped on either side of a strip that runs through the center. Both are equally panty melting.

Knowing he has to be the one to come to terms with our play, I wait for him to address me. The ball's in his court.

A groan disperses, full lips purse, and forehead crinkles as he glares at the phallic toy.

A hardy erection is outlined down his pant leg.

Rob's shirt expands as he takes in a deep breath, punishing the cotton fibers.

The thick ropes of his tattooed forearms contract and release as he fights his inner struggle. He doesn't have full-sleeve tats, only forearm ones, and a large eagle spanning his shoulders—a homage to his twenty years in the service.

I scratch my nail along the armrest, waiting, observing... soaking up his presence like an addict.

"Fuck!" Another step back.

His cock flexes the tiniest of movements as a small stain of pre-cum bleeds through the denim, turning it darker in that single spot.

I lick my lips at the hotness of it all, my own heart rate rising, clit aching.

Rob places both of his hands behind his neck, fingers interlacing, his biceps bulging. "I dunno if I can do this, baby. I just... fuck!"

"We've got all night," I reassure, knowing that Tyler won't contact us unless we reach out to him first. He respects our time together.

"You listened to him. You're gonna make me ride that." He juts his chin toward the dildo.

"I never make you do anything."

"Bullshit," he snarls.

See what I said about his walls? This is when

things get real interesting.

"It is true that I wanna see your sweet, sweet, hole riding that cock for me. That I want you to let your guard down so I can spend time with my Big Guy."

"I'm not a fag," an echoing bark.

"Never said you were." My tone's serene. As I said, I'm a Rob expert. I expect this resistance every session.

"Why do you do this to me?" he accuses.

"I'm not doing anything. Don't lie to yourself, Rob, you like to play with me." I exude the utmost patience. Even if his words sometimes hurt, I don't let it show... Can't. He doesn't want to be this way. It's not his fault he bears deep seeded emotional scars.

Rob shakes his head defiantly, neck cracking through the violent back and forth. "It's a sin, Ronan. A sin."

"What is?"

"All of it." As a mask of agony wrinkles his handsome face, he waves his hand, gesturing to me, to the room, himself, his boner. The mature lines around his eyes accentuate more than before, adding to his struggle. If I could make it all go away, I would. But this is a process.

"We waited too long between sessions again, didn't we?" I ask.

"We always do. I don't fuckin' like her in my head. Her voice. Her... fuck! You fix it. You always do. I don't wanna be fucked up." Self-hatred, agony, and bone-deep resentment wafts off him in potent waves.

"I know you don't, so say it. Say what you need to say. Let it out." I brace myself for the word vomit that's to come. It will sting like a bullwhip lancing my heart. It usually does. However, I can take it. I'm a strong woman, and this isn't about me. This is about Rob and his demons.

"I fucked five women since our last session. Five. I ripped open their cunts with my cock, and they begged me for it. They cried out my name. They wanted me, Ronan, they wanted this." To cement his statement, Rob grips his hard-on like he's disgusted with its presence.

Swallowing down the bile that burns my throat, I gather my inner strength, expression impassive. I can't lie and say our arrangement doesn't sometimes make me jealous, or break my heart, because it does. But, what kind of hypocrite would I be if I forbade him from fulfilling his needs, when I always fulfill mine? Rob can't get the ruthless fucking out of his system by using me as his outlet. Our relationship doesn't function on that level. I wish it did. Trust me, we tried and failed time and time again. He still resorts to club chicks. Still has to have some degree of control. Our level of intimacy prevents him from reaching that mindless pleasure, where he can go blank for a while—unfeeling. Once we breach that intimate threshold he can't switch it off. And if I submit to him, to let him screw me like all the other women, he literally vomits from guilt. Multiple times. At one point, after a particularly emotionless session, he was ill for a week. It took us another ten days to get our relationship back on track. Since then, we've given up meeting all of his needs in our unique partnership.

"You're mad. Fuck. I... You know I don't want to

be like this, baby. I... shit." Overcome with emotion, Rob stares at the ceiling and blinks slowly, Adam's apple bobbing in his throat. The glassiness of his eyes catches the overhead lights.

"I'm not mad. I promise." I do the little criss-cross thing atop my heart and pretend to stick a needle in my eye.

He sighs.

I sigh.

A pregnant silence descends as Rob collects his waning composure.

I let it be. No need to rush it.

Does the thought of him screwing five different women make me want to bash my head into the nearest wall? Yeppers, it sure does. Can I get over it? Yes, I can. I've been doing this for half a decade. If we can overcome that, we can certainly navigate this.

I re-cross my legs in the opposite direction, the crease behind my knee damp from sitting so long.

Rob turns around, his back to me, then reaches over his shoulder, fists a section of the shirt, and tears it over his head in one sexy tug. I have to bite my lip to keep from groaning when he exposes all that thick ruggedness. Rob isn't like those young, super-cut gym rats. He's tall, tattooed, tanned, and rocks the silver fox vibe to a nipple-hardening T. All of his muscles are defined under a thin layer of I-still-like-to-eat-pizza-pasta-and-pussy.

To lighten the atmosphere, I catcall like a naughty construction worker.

Rob chuckles and faces me again, grinning at my silliness. He runs a hand down his pecs and abs. "Does somebody like?" He winks, crimson dabbing his cheeks.

"Oh, I likey. I likey a lot." Adding to the charade, I rub my palms together like a greedy housewife wanting some tube steak for dinner and crack a devious, half-cocked smile.

The stain on Rob's jeans grows.

I must be getting to him. Chipping away little by little.

Because he can't help himself, Rob rolls a nipple between his fingers. That's one way to get his motor running on all cylinders.

"I am sorry, Ronan, about all of it. I wish I could be different."

"I know ya do. That's why I always say there's no room for guilt in our playroom. Now tell me what you want me to do to you tonight without backing down. How does it make you feel that I wanna see you fall apart on that cock?" It makes me hot thinking about it. I'm kind of addicted to the whole femdom aspect of my life. There's a heady power behind it.

"Dirty. It feels fuckin' dirty," Rob growls, his upper lip curled into a handsome snarl that I want to suck on.

"Do you wanna be dirty with me, Big Man?" I purr, tracing a fingertip across the sweetheart neckline of my teddy to seduce him.

Clearly affected by my teasing, he samples his bottom lip leaving a wet sheen in its wake. "What I need and what I feel are two different things."

"It's not a sin, sweetheart, to embrace pleasure with me because we love each other."

"So everyone says."

"What do you say?"

Rob's eyelids slide closed in a way that speaks of arousal, not unease. A richer gruffness tinges his tone. "I say, I always wanna be dirty with you. That I wanna feel you and fuck you like a slut, bent over, gasping like the club whores."

I'd love that, too, once in a while. Being screwed like a boneless ragdoll has its appeal.

"And why's that?"

"'Cause it aches, all the time."

"What aches?" I think I know.

He thumps a meaty fist on his breastplate. "Bein' away from you. Goin' through this same fuckin' do-si-do week after week. Not gettin' any better."

"Did you throw up after having sex with them?"

A stiff nod. "Twice."

"That's progress."

He shrugs unconvinced. "Not really."

At least his hostility has died, and we can be candid with each other. That's a step in the right direction. Whether he believes it or not, puking twice is favorable compared to the five or more that could've happened. It's about perspective. The therapist he sees twice a month thinks Rob unconsciously tries to purge what his subconscious believes are sins by throwing up. It's also a unique form of unwanted self-flagellation. To combat part of his inner struggles, he exercises, rides, and works with criminals that he doesn't have to be polite around. Every facet of Rob's life is constructed in a way to heal him or provide healthy outlets for his issues. I'm also one of the outlets; the one that tries to fix his sexual responses. At first, we couldn't hug without strain, cursing, and rage. Obviously, he's overcome much more than that since. Baby steps.

"Why don't you take off the rest of your clothes for me?" It's a soft order. One that he can reject, but I don't think he will. The tension has bled from his system, the teddy bear I cherish is ready to play whether he realizes it or not.

Fists down at his sides, Rob shuffles his feet. "I dunno if I'm ready."

"You are." A bit firmer.

"Fuck."

"Pants, Big Man. Show me that thick cock."

A flash of panic and uncertainty morphs his face for a suspended moment before he flips open his belt buckle, and undoes the button on his jeans using two deft fingers. Carefully, he retracts the zipper and shoves the denim along with boxer briefs to his ankles. Bent in half, the muscles in his shoulders flex as he unlaces his boots, and removes them with his socks and bundle of clothing. A small sigh flutters through the air. Returning to full height, Rob kicks the pile to the wayside and stares at me full on. His massive dick sways back and forth like a baseball bat—happy to be uncaged.

Giddy beyond belief, yet careful not to smile, I harness my cool Mistress vibe instead, and tip my forehead toward the dildo, and bottle of lube beside it.

Rob's Adam's apple rolls in his throat as he swallows, fighting off nerves. It shouldn't be sexy but is.

"Talk to me," I encourage to keep him out of his head.

"I'm gonna kick Tyler's scrawny ass for suggesting

this," Rob grits through clenched teeth, taking a tentative step in the right direction.

"Why?" I snicker.

Exhaling loudly, a rumble percolating in his chest, Rob scratches the back of his neck, shaking his head. "Because that fucker suggested a big plug, puttin' the idea in your head. That dildo wouldn't be an anal wrecker if it weren't for that little shit." He doesn't seem the least bit pissed about it. If anything, he's now amused.

"How do you know?" His mind fascinates me. Aside from Rob's sexual hang-ups, he sees the world differently than most. He's more honest, raw, and doesn't wear blinders, whereas Tyler's a bit of a dreamer.

He scratches his elbow. "'Cause I do. Your small cheek twitch is a tell. You're fightin' off a smile or laugh, not sure which. I think you forget I work with bad guys who make it their job to lie for sport. Your expressions say a lot, even when you're trying hard not to have one."

See. Brilliant mind. He's spot on.

I shift again, more turned on by his observations than I should be. Dommes are supposed to take pride in their ability to control their outward emotions. But most of us don't have human lie detectors assessing our every move. He's been reading me since the moment he stepped through the door. It's a heady feeling when you think about it.

I try hard not to squirm again under his scrutiny that fills my veins with lust.

"What else does my body language say?" My bare toes curl in anticipation.

"Well..." The smart-ass taps his chin, scanning me every which way for show. "Your stiff nipples say you're aroused. The subtle squirm you fail at hiding suggests anxiety, or that you wanna jump my bones. I'm gonna go with the latter. Your eyelids hood the slightest when I say something that makes you wet... like right now. You love that I can read you like a sexy fuckin' book."

"I do. A lot." This time I don't suppress the salacious grin. There's no use.

Rob's brow quirks like Dwayne Johnson and I almost come on the spot. "Am I wrong?"

Jesus Christ, he's too much. My hottie's in rare form tonight—flirty, open, and less combative.

"About which part?" I ask.

"All of it." He takes a step closer.

"What do you think?"

"I think you want to keep me talkin', 'cause I keep takin' steps toward this anus destroyer, not away. The thought of me riding it makes you hot. And you love that Tyler put the thought in your head."

"Why would I love that?"

"'Cause it keeps us interconnected, right where you want us to be. It's like he's here, cheering us on."

"Does that bother you?"

Half a shrug. "Ehhh... Honestly? A bit. But not for the reason you might think. Tyler and I, as you know, share a weird-as-fuck bond—obviously. 'Cause him sendin' a picture of a plug in his ass would gross out most straight men. It gets to me because it doesn't cause that reaction."

"So none of that ever grosses you out?"

"Nope. Not really. You're an extension of me, and

by way of that, he is also."

"But you don't feel that way about Kendra."

"Kendra doesn't have your heart. We do. I've seen, been through, and heard a fuckuvalot in my life. Ninety-five percent of the time I can identify fact from fiction. Fact is we're yours. And, our unit has grown stronger since Tyler came into the picture. Not weaker, like I had suspected it might three years ago."

"You're goin' deep tonight, Big Man."

"Monday's gonna come soon enough, and there's no reason to go into any discussion without layin' the cards on the table. The ones I can, at least."

"Are you nervous about 'the talk'?" I air-quote for emphasis.

"Not today. Maybe tomorrow I will be. I'm too busy tryin' to figure out how I'm gonna get that thing inside me without havin' an episode." He inclines his head in the toy's direction, lips pressed into a thin, contemplative line.

"You've ridden those before."

"Not that big."

"You like 'em... not small." Using the word big doesn't sound right. Rob has a hard enough time coming to terms with his love of anal sex. Emphasizing his preference in a grotesque manner won't keep the demons locked up in their compartmentalized cells. Subtlety is key.

Another step closer to the dildo, eyes locked on its offending size. "There's pushing limits, Mistress, and then there's that."

Ah, yes, there it is, that sweet word imparting his lips—Mistress.

Whether Rob admits it aloud or not, the size turns him on. I special ordered this toy for him months ago, and have been waiting for the right time to use it. I even consulted Tyler on the purchase. He has good taste. The navy-blue color is masculine enough. We didn't go flesh tone since I felt it hovers a little closer to the bi line if it looks real. The ten-and-a-half-inch length is a monster, not too far from his own girthy eight incher. Where it gets crazy is the circumference. The average man is four and a half inches around when erect. Rob is closer to six, I think. This monstrosity is eight. Not the largest by any stretch, in a sex toy industry that caters to the wild and crazy without batting an eyelash, but it does go well beyond normal parameters.

"I think it's the perfect size for you. A big dick for a big man."

Rob groans, scrubbing a shaky palm down his face.

"You don't think so?" I smirk, reveling in his adorable discomfort.

"I think you're my Mistress who likes to test me."

"That's part of the fun."

He snorts. "For you."

"For both of us. Now go on and lube it up for me... nice and slow."

Another groan reverberates as my man reaches the dildo and kneels. Without protest, he clicks open the bottle of flavored lube. With Rob and Tyler I prefer this kind, just in case I get the urge to rim them. Regular lube doesn't have a pleasant flavor. Strawberry, on the other hand, is palatable. Pouring a generous amount on the tip of the rubber cock, it cascades down the veiny sides.

Rob glances up at me, the thick muscles in his neck bulging as he wraps a fist around the toy. My fingers can't touch around its girth, yet Rob's can—barely. Up and down, not making a sound aside from his harsh pants, and the wet schlick-schlick of lube, he readies it. I grow wetter at the sight. There's something extra hot about a big guy on his knees, stroking a fake dick while his own stands proud between beefy thighs. A dribble of pre-cum runs down the underside of his prick.

"Does it feel good?" I purr, spreading my legs to give him a front-row view of my glistening snatch.

Rob watches my deliberate movements, licking his lips as if starved for a taste.

When he doesn't reply, I try again. "Does the cock feel good?"

"Uh huh," he mumbles, jacking the dildo faster, eyes locked on my cunt. Deep inside the recesses of my depraved mind, I imagine it's Tyler's member deriving pleasure from him. We've never played together before, but I do dream of it often. Sometimes it's them touching, sharing in mutual gratification as I watch. Others, it's us together—me as the center of their universe. If it wouldn't spook Rob, I'd roll play the naughty scenes flashing in my head. One in which Tyler begs for our touch. Not mine—ours.

A flutter dances in my belly at the mere notion.

No.

I shove that delusion into a mental trash compactor.

Now's not the time to fantasize. Later, maybe,

when I'm alone.

Readjusting my braid over my shoulder, I blink twice and focus on the present.

It's show time.

"Prep yourself," I command, my voice raspy with anticipation. Doesn't he look incredible, stroking, stroking, stroking that monster, priming it for insertion? I think he does. Beyond freaking sexy.

I bite my bottom lip as Rob reopens the lube with his thumb, and pours a liberal amount on his fingertips. Reaching behind himself, I witness the very moment he delves inside. A sharp wince covers his handsome face half a second before it goes slack. A wave of euphoria washes over him, blocking out all the bad juju. That's it, sweetheart, get in there, and explore your hole. It's not a sin.

A faint moan emits as Rob rocks back to finger himself.

"That's it, babe. How's it feel?"

His eyelids shutter and chin drops to chest. "Fuck, Mistress, just... fuck."

The ache in my clit and breasts intensifies as I watch him in action. The loud squelch of Rob fucking that tight hole is too much to bear, so I moan alongside him, dropping a hand to my pussy. It's pointless to tease myself, I'm too revved up to care. Eyes on my man, I drive two fingers into the honeypot.

Yes!

My chest heaves skyward, head snapping back as I cry out for him.

Answering my call, Rob straddles the dildo, positions it, then does the magical burn and slide. It's glorious to watch, every single throbbing second.

The monster breaches his outer ring. I don't have to see it firsthand to know. The spotlight overhead illuminating Rob's face illustrates it all. The lip-biting grimace, the subtle hip adjustment, followed by the blissful acceptance into his body. It's a gluttonous eye feast to behold.

An inch is inserted, and he's already panting, cheeks flushed, pecs glistening with a thin sheen of sweat. I can practically see his heart thundering in that perfect chest.

Sucked into the moment, into him—us, I batter my g-spot in a series of jabs.

"That's so hot," I breathe, hooking a knee over the arm of the chair for better access. I add a third finger. The extra stretch is just what I need, as I watch my man come apart.

Palms lying flat on both knees, Rob nods his response.

"How's it feel?"

"Full," he chokes, beads of perspiration rolling down the side of his face. "So fuckin' full."

"Do you like it?"

I know he does.

"Yes," he says on a whiskey-tinged growl.

That's it? That's all he's gonna give me is a meager yes? That's not good enough.

Tsking his lack of response, I arch a brow. "Where're your manners, Big Guy?"

"Thank you, Mistress," he rasps.

"What are you thanking me for?"

Ignoring my question, Rob sinks another two inches, filling his channel. A guttural moan ejects his parted lips, air freezes in his lungs, blunt fingernails imbed in his muscular thighs as he curls them under. A violent tremor takes over his frame. Oh, yes, he loves that cock in his ass, perhaps more than I do.

"Do you wanna fuck that beautiful hole for your Mistress?"

"Yes." He nods rapidly, lost in the moment.

Nope. That's not going to do. When I ask a question, I expect a proper reply.

Unsatisfied by his monosyllabic answers, I kneel on the floor in front of the chair. Placing both hands on the cool hardwood, I position myself on all fours and crawl toward Rob like a lioness tracking her prey. Our eyes lock, tethering us as one, while my hips swish gracefully between movements. Uncupped, my breasts sway in the lace, nipples grazing the fabric, turning me on more than I already am.

Halfway to Rob, I pause to dispense another order. "More."

Gulping, he blinks a slow yes, head dipping the slightest in submission. Then it happens, that insane body surrenders to the invader, taking more shaft.

Those glistening eyes roll back into his skull.

"Good job, Big Guy," I praise because that's what he deserves. Not many people would fend off their demons like Rob does. Even less would trust their woman enough to know what's best for them. This is what he needs today. To feel loved, taken care of, pleasure, and respect. I respect his body enough to know what it can and can't take. What it desires and doesn't.

It's time to amp up my game.

Arriving at my man, I don't say anything as I

nudge his dick with my nose. Rob shivers. I grin, and do it again. A faint moan is my gift. I sample the crown with the poke of my tongue, delighting in the scent of man, spicy cologne, and the fresh outdoors that swirls inside my nose, intoxicating my senses. It's utterly divine. An aphrodisiac in its own right. Another sweep of my tongue and the slight tang of his pre-cum awakens my taste buds. Yes. That's exactly what I need. I do it once more, and my stomach shudders, nipples throbbing, as I suppress the urge to reach back and finger myself in tandem with my kitten licks.

"Oh. Fuck!" Rob's hands fist on his thighs, knuckles blanching. I sample him again, watching the tension in his forearms surge out of my periphery. He loves this alright. To get a better reaction, I suckle that mushroom head in my mouth—not too hard, not too soft, just enough to drive him wild.

Ahhh, yes, there's that full-body quake.

A broken moan and shuddery exhale.

My own wetness begins to trickle down the insides of my thighs. If I don't get off soon, I'm gonna have a severe case of lady blue balls. I need him so damn bad, and he doesn't even know it.

Squeezing my lips around his thickness, a burst of pre-cum bathes my tongue, and I swallow it down with a hungry groan.

Wanting more, I grip the space where his thighs meet pelvis and shove him downward, forcing his body to impale itself on the dildo, as far as it can go. Rob doesn't stop me. He obeys the silent order without resistance.

"Ronan! Mistress!" he roars, taking it all. "Fu-ck.

Fuck! Fuck!"

Jesus, I can't take it anymore. Those sounds. His taste—the heady smell of his pre-cum... I...

Throwing caution to the wind, I pull away from his glans, push Rob's hands off his thighs, and straddle that sexy lap. Feet planted flat on the floor, I thread my fingers behind his neck and sink to the hilt on that monster dick. Then, I come. Hard. It's unexpected and so fucking powerful that stars burst behind my eyelids. Incoherent sobs of relief pour from my lips. Rob palms my ass cheeks and forces me to ride him through the crescendo. But it doesn't let up. One orgasm ebbs as the next slams into me like a bolt of lightning. Unable to stop, I hold on for dear life as my pussy clamps around its mate.

"Rob!" I wail before sinking my teeth into his throat to gain some traction—marking him. It doesn't work. They keep coming and I... dammit!

Rob grunts, impaling me on explosive repeat.

"I'm so sorry," I cry out, sagging against his chest, giving my body what it wants—him.

"I got you, Mistress."

"I needed it too much. Needed you too much."

He kisses my cheek. "I know."

"D-don't come, too."

"I won't."

"Promise?"

"I promise."

And he doesn't. For God knows how long, Rob helps fuck me on his cock as he rides the dildo. I climax. We moan together. I peak again. We embrace each other. Somewhere along the way our lips fuse, tongues tangling in a sweet caress. Not once does my

Big Man let his doubts creep in. Not once do I become a faceless slut. I'm his, and he's mine as we bask in the pleasure our bodies create—in the love we share.

Licking his swollen bottom lip, I pry my mouth away from Rob's, panting to catch my breath. My forehead drops to his damp shoulder. I'm wrung out, pussy pleasantly sore. "I can't believe I let that happen," I grouse, cheeks flaming hot with embarrassment.

"Sex with Tyler the other night was cut short, wasn't it?"

"Yes. How did you know?"

"Because you're needier, less focused when you've gone without our cocks for too long." Aside from his rough sandpaper voice, Rob doesn't seem bothered by this in the slightest. He should be. I broke the scene. And I never do that. Ever. This isn't like me at all. It's bad enough that I come half the time as soon as they enter me. Who does that? Me. With Tyler this week, that was forgivable. I'd been stretched to my limit, as was he. Neither of us lasted. Tonight… Sheesh…

Wrapping my arms around his torso in a hug, I nuzzle my nose in the crook of Rob's freshly marred neck. "I feel like a fraud."

"Nobody's perfect, Ronan." He runs a steady palm down my spine, soothing me when I don't deserve it. "Not even our Mistress. You can't let yourself get this bad again."

"I thought Kendra satisfied me enough."

"Kendra isn't us. She doesn't have a dick or your heart."

"I know. But shit...this is mortifying."

Rob chuckles. Freaking chuckles, even though his cock is still as hard as stone inside me. Reaching behind him, he snags the corner of his pant leg and drags the denim closer. Then he digs into a pocket and pulls out his cell phone. A few taps on the screen later and I hear... Tyler's voice.

"Rob, what's goin' on? Aren't you two supposed to be in session?"

I clam up not wanting to talk to them about this.

"We are."

I don't have to look to know Rob's panning over our bodies for Tyler to see.

There's a distinct groan through video chat. "You're having sex already?"

"We weren't supposed to," I mumble into Rob's neck, wanting to disappear.

"Next time you two have a short night of sex, you gotta stay to give her more in the mornin'."

"Why? What's wrong?" Tyler asks, way too concerned.

"She kinda jumped me tonight. Couldn't help herself."

"Did you say, jumped you? You mean like she did to me last year when you went on vacation?"

"Yeah."

"I hate you both so damn much right now," I complain. Why do they have to go and bring that up? We agreed never to speak of it again. I'd had another moment of weakness, it's not like it happens all the time.

Enjoying my discomfort way too much, Rob full-on body laughs and relays my grievance to Tyler, since he can't read my lips in this position.

My sexy artist joins in on Rob's amusement with a hearty chuckle of his own.

"I'm never having sex with you again." I nip Rob's neck to cement my silly declaration. His cock flexes inside me, ruining any progress I've made to stay mad at them. Why do they have to be so darn attractive, and have such nice dicks? Add their personalities into the mix, and I'm a goner. It's not fair. Truly. I rule over numerous men in a given week, none of which tempt me like they do. Not even Bonez, one of the hottest subs I've ever worked with.

Rob pats my butt affectionately, dropping an equally nice kiss to the side of my head.

"I can't believe you called Tyler," I whisper hiss.

The jerks. All of them.

"He's better with this emotional stuff than I am."

I want to argue that's not true, but it is.

"Ronan, we're not your clients. You're allowed to let go sometimes. We're okay with that," my hot masochist reasons.

That's not true. What if Rob couldn't handle it? What if he had an episode? That would've been my fault. I would have provoked it. The last thing I want is him throwing up after sex, or worse. Trust me, there's been way worse. Sure, it hasn't happened in a few years, but it has happened. With the strides he's made, I can't stomach the thought of him relapsing like that again. Not with me.

"Yeah. What he said," Rob agrees, still hard, still his teddy bear self.

Sighing, I sit up to see Tyler's handsome face staring back at me from the phone.

"It wasn't on purpose," I speak aloud, not signing for Rob's benefit. He doesn't know much ASL.

Tyler replies a firm, "Doesn't matter if it was."

"He's riding the dildo. The blue one." I'm pretty sure that's what did me in.

Tyler's large lips form into a shocked "O." "The one we picked out for him?"

I nod. "The same one."

"Fuuck." Moaning like he's in pain, Rob hands me the cell, and drops his own forehead to my shoulder, massive arms wrapping around me in a vise.

Um... okay. That's weird.

"What's wrong?" I card my fingers through his short hair as Tyler and I watch our Big Guy with concern.

"Is he okay?" Tyler asks, brows furrowed, blue eyes radiating warmth.

I shrug.

Rob's cock jerks at the sound of Tyler's voice. "Please don't move," he croaks.

"What? Why?"

"'Cause I'm gonna come if you do."

Giving Rob a second to reel in whatever's going on inside his head, I mouth to Tyler, "He said he's going to come."

"You think it's because of the dildo?" he signs.

"Maybe?"

"You think he likes that we both picked it out for him?"

"Would you?"

"Hell yes, I would. You're my partners."

Interesting.

"Big Man, you doing alright?" Tyler asks out loud,

winking at me with a grin.

"Shut up, boy," Rob grunts in distress. "This is all your fault."

I relay the sentiment to boy, and he laughs a light, chest-rumbling sound that heats me from the inside out. My heart gives a little kick.

Following by example, I expel my own muted giggle. Rob joins in too with a growl of frustration. I cup the back of his neck and turn my face in to land a peck.

"No coming," I remind, lips skimming the side of his head.

"Then both of you, shut up."

"Are our voices the problem, babe? Wouldn't it be better if I got up?" I'm part serious, part teasing. This is kinda fun.

"Fuck no."

Embracing my Domme side, no longer ashamed, I clench around Rob's girth and lean my weight forward to force that dildo further up his canal, testing his obedience.

Rob's fingers dig into my back, as short puffs of moist air bathe the side of my neck. Yet, he doesn't make a peep. Not one. He must be concentrating. That's either a good sign or bad, if he goes to a dark place.

Determined to push his limits further in a positive direction, I rotate my hips in small circles. Still no reaction. Oh boy, that won't do. Needing the use of both hands, I blow Tyler a kiss goodbye and end the chat. He'll understand. He always does.

Setting the phone on the ground, I take control of our unbalanced situation. Unlatching my man's arms from around me, he grumbles his displeasure but doesn't put up a fight. To reset the tone where it should've been all along, I carefully dismount his erection. Rob doesn't like that one bit when a full-fledged shudder overtakes his body, testing his restraint. Those gorgeous eyes slam shut as his clenched fists jab into the tops of his thighs, biceps flexing.

"It's okay, sweetheart," I whisper, not wanting to make matters worse.

A low rumble is his reply.

Dropping his head forward, rivulets of sweat pour down Rob's pinched face. I hope this is him battling an orgasm, not something worse. Maybe Tyler and I were wrong. Maybe Rob didn't like that we picked out the toy for him. I don't think that's true. However, I haven't seen him this edgy during a scene in three years. And it's never been like this before.

Treading lightly, I rest on my knees in front of him, ass perched on feet.

Minutes tick by with no resolution in sight.

His jaw doesn't unlock. Nor does the coiled tension in Rob's shoulders dissipate the slightest. I want to instruct him to remove the toy from his bottom, to get relief if that's what's causing his torment. But I'm afraid to speak. For all I know he's reliving years of psychological abuse in his mind. My parents were free-spirited hippies; I have no firsthand experience of what he's endured. Only that I respect his past and will always nurture our future, one step at a time. Even when it gets tough, like now, when I'm left navigating in the dark.

Rob's breathing intensifies and legs begin to

shake.

His cock is so hard it could hammer railroad spikes up and down the Florida coastline.

What's going on inside that mysterious head of yours, handsome?

Knowing I can't ask that aloud and get a coherent response, I do the only thing I know how to do. I grab the bottle of lube, click open the top, drizzle a fair amount into my palm, reclose the cap, then warm the liquid by rubbing my hands together, spreading it around. Rob doesn't peek to see what I'm up to. Something about this doesn't sit right in my stomach, and I can't help but feel like it's my fault.

Quit it, Ronan, now's not the time for guilt.

Closing my eyes, I center myself and focus on the task at hand—Operation Fix the Big Guy. My fear has no place here. We've been through far worse. I can do this. I can salvage our time together. This wouldn't be the first time I've had to think outside the box. I pretty much do that every day.

A final exhale, and I'm ready to test the invisible limits. Pray, I don't screw this up.

Leaning forward the slightest bit, I wrap both hands tightly around his boner, and the response is immediate.

"Ronan!" Rob roars, raspy and raw.

That's better than nothing, Big Guy. I'll take what I can get.

Determined to see this through, I jack that piece of meat in long, strong, moan-inducing strokes. And what beautiful moans they are. Wild and cantankerous ones that are filled with equal parts rage and lust, love and hate, pleasure and pain.

Those expressive eyes snap open on the next upward tug, and lock on me, silently begging for something I can't put my finger on. No words are exchanged as I watch my man begin to fray apart at the seams. Pre-cum leaks from Rob's slit, adding to the lube. His body succumbs to its baser needs, pulse throbbing through my fingertips. The heat of his gaze sears straight through me. Yep, he wants this. I can feel it deep in my soul. This is us getting back to the basics. Back to us, where he needs to be.

It's time to retake the upper hand.

"Ride it," I order.

Submitting without protest, Rob shamelessly fucks himself on the dildo, as I edge him closer to the brink of no return.

"Play with your nipples," a sterner command.

Eyes tipping back into his skull, those fists unfold from Rob's thighs to do what I know he craves. Thumb and forefingers work in tandem to twist and pluck those sharp points 'til he is lost in the labyrinth of ecstasy.

"Fuck!" he bellows between moans.

That's it.

I drive him to the precipice.

Rob stills on the toy, yet I stroke him faster, smiling at the magnificent sight before me. I'm going to wreck him. Mark him with my touch, and my love, until he no longer knows what's sin and what's not.

Heavy balls coated in a light dusting of gray-black pubes draw up to his groin.

Yes. We're almost there.

I lick my lips, jonesing to taste the steady stream of pre-cum that bathes my hand, as Rob's head shoots back in a broken war cry.

"No," I bark. "You don't give me that cum 'til I say you can."

"Ronan," he growls in ultimate frustration, lungs starving for oxygen.

"Not. Yet."

To assert that I'm in charge, I increase my tempo, fists flying over his cock in a blur. Jesus, I wanna ride that big thing again. But I can't—won't. I already got mine, more than once. This isn't about me. This is about him.

"Not much longer. You're doing so good, sweetheart," I praise.

Damn, this is a workout.

My arms start to burn from exertion, but I power through. No pain no gain. It's all worth it just to watch him glisten like a Greek God underneath the spotlight. I knew it was the best choice for tonight's scene.

Rob's abs clench, the muscles in his thighs bulging. He pinches those nipples harder like he can't stop even if he tried.

"Ronan," he grits, riding the dildo in short bursts.

"Not yet."

"Fuck!"

"Say it."

"Fuck!"

I jack his crown, thumbs paying extra special attention to his frenulum between strokes.

All the air heaves from his lungs, and I know it's now or never.

Rob's eyes latch onto mine, vulnerable and powerless, glistening in limbo.

"I love you," he groans, bottom lip trembling.

My heart explodes in a bomb of pink, dick-shaped glitter.

Smiling so brightly my cheeks hurt, I dip my head in silent permission, and Rob doesn't hesitate to release everything. Nostrils flaring wide, spine arching, head thrown back, cum rockets out of his shaft in thick bursts of white as disjointed moans pour freely from his soul.

Yes. That's it. Absolute perfection.

I tug him a few more times, to wring the last of his orgasm out, before Rob sags forward, going half boneless.

I prop his damp forehead on my shoulder, and caress his back, not caring that my hands are coated in jizz and lube. That's what showers are for. "You did great."

He presses an open-mouthed kiss to my collarbone. "I'm... damn."

"I know. And thank you."

"Babe, don't thank me for sayin' that."

"You know I have to." Only because I realize how difficult it is for him to admit. I'm the only person in his life, aside from his son, who's heard those words spoken aloud. That in itself is a miracle. When it first happened years ago, I cried. It touched me beyond words, as it always does each and every time he declares it. It awakens something in me that solidifies our bond, tethering us. It reminds me why my soul chose him in the first place. Before Rob, I never believed in true love and all that fairytale mumbo jumbo. Since, I've become a believer in lots of things I never put much thought to in the first place.

"No, you don't. I should be able to say those words other times too, not only when I'm about to nut."

"You'll get there."

"I do, though, ya know."

"Love me?"

"Uh huh."

"I know you do." I press my own kiss to the side of his sweaty head and let it linger there for a handful of heartbeats.

"Even if I can't say it most of the time. It's always there," he whispers to my neck.

"I believe you."

"Do ya think Tyler does?"

"Know that you love me, or him?"

"Both... maybe... fuck... I dunno."

"It's okay to love him, Big Man."

"It's not the same."

"However you choose to love someone is your business, not mine. I'm not going to judge you for how you feel no matter what. You know this."

"I know, babe. I know. Now let's go lie down. My poor hole needs a break."

Severing our embrace, both of us still on our knees, Rob kisses my forehead before he dismounts the dildo.

"Dammn," he groans, climbing to his feet.

Staying on the floor to get a better look, I tap the side of his hip as he stretches every which way to unkink his muscles. "Show me."

Knowing exactly what I'm referring to, Rob turns around and spreads his insanely hot glutes to give me an up-close-and-personal view of his hole. And what a magnificent view it is. The rim's red and puffy, slick with lube. What's even sexier is the dilation. Drawn to that forbidden place like a moth to a flame, I trace my fingertip around the crinkly edge.

"Babe," Rob moans all whiskey and gravel.

"Just a minute. I need to see it."

"You're doin' more than that," he croaks.

If I could see his face, I'd bet good money he's blushing.

"I wanna taste it, too." And I do. So very bad. He might've gotten his rocks off, but I'm still hungry for more. What can I say? I'm insatiable when it comes to my men.

"Mistress. I... fuck."

"Are you saying I can't?"

Rob's thick fingers imbed deeper in his cheeks, on the verge of bruising skin. I think someone's struggling a little with what I want to do to him. It's not often he lets me lick him there. Out of courtesy I always ask first, since I know how delicate this situation is.

"I... didn't...sa-say that."

Greenlight.

My mouth waters.

Rising up onto my knees, I rest my hands over Rob's that are doing such a nice job keeping him wide for me. Then, I swipe the flat of my tongue across that puffy ring and moan like it's the best thing I've tasted in years. Strawberries and man...Mmmmm.

"You're delicious."

A slight tremble and cute fumble of words are his response.

Powerless to curb the aching need any longer, I return a hand to my pussy and go to town on it. In and out I pound myself as I eat that nicely prepped hole. Even the inside is nice and slick against my tongue, ready to be devoured thanks to his handy prep work before our session. God, I know most people don't get off on eating ass, but when you have such a fine specimen to ravish it's impossible not to salivate over. So I don't even try.

Burying my face between his cheeks, I lick, and tongue fuck his hole until I'm moaning like a whore, and coming all over my fingers in a rush of shameless debauchery.

When I'm finished getting my fill, I pull away, swipe the wetness from my mouth with the back of my hand, and all but melt into the floor. Flopping onto my back, sated to my core, the coolness of the hardwood beneath me is a welcome relief on my otherwise overheated flesh.

Rob turns around, smiling down at me, his erection swaying in the wind, face bright red. His cupid's bow is swollen from chewing it too hard.

Slow and seductively I lick my lips for show. "Your ass is..." I groan unabashed, eyes rolling back, lids fluttering to express how amazing it is to me.

Rob shifts on his feet, shy and oh so adorable. Which is very unlike the badass biker we all know and love. This is my teddy bear that lives deep within. The part of Rob that's often insecure and unsure. It's one of his many facets that I cherish the most.

Needing him closer, I crook a finger to have my man join me, and he does. Kneeling, Rob lays his chest atop mine, and fuses our mouths together in a sensual, all-consuming kiss, that flows on and on with no destination in sight. Shifting a bit, he slots himself between my thighs, and I wrap my calves around him, locking my feet at the small of his back. My arms hook around Rob's neck as he drops to his elbows on either side of me. That fine cock nudges my entrance, and I wordlessly urge him inside with the press of my heels. There, that's it, what we both needed; connected in all ways possible, where we can just be with one another. No sex. No fucking. No more scenes. No Mistress and submissive. No sin. Only Rob and Ronan exploring each other's mouths, lost in passion.

This is it. The moment I've never been happier in all my life... to love and be loved by two perfectly imperfect men. This is what real fairytales look like. Princesses have got nothing on us.

7

MAY THE TRUTH SET YOU FREE

Monday

The scent of homemade manicotti and garlic bread suffuses the air in the central part of the house as the doorbell rings. Wearing a black, knee-length, cotton dress, pantyless and barefoot, I skip like an over-excited schoolgirl to answer the buzzer. It has to be one of my men. Tonight's the night we talk business. Not the real kind, but of a personal nature. Tyler has been on me about this for months, and I've finally relented for all of our sakes.

The doorbell chimes again as I stop to double-check my appearance in the entry mirror. My long, black, curly hair has been tamed tonight and tumbles in loose waves down my back. I dabbed on a subtle smoky eye, a wing-tipped liner, Va-Va-Voom mascara to plump my otherwise lifeless eyelashes, and a ruby-red lip with gloss overlay—classic. I'm going for love and comfort, not over the top Hollywood glamour. I want them to feel welcome in my home. It's cozy and warm, not magazine chic. Unless the magazine wanted to do an expose on the world's largest Tyler Coopman art collection. I do own more of those than anyone in existence, including the man himself. He isn't fond of displaying his own creations in his drab apartment. The gallery he part owns houses less than ten Tyler Coopman masterpieces at a time. Not because he doesn't want them there, but they sell out too fast to keep them stocked...

Ugh, I'm deflecting, aren't I?

Can you tell I'm anxious?

Satisfied with my appearance, I unlock the door and pull it open, only to be caught off guard. Clutching my chest, I laugh awkwardly at the sight of both men standing on my stoop side by side. Tyler, as always, is outfitted in a pair of skinny jeans with holes in the knees, and a screen-printed shirt with paint speckles by the hem. Attached to the hand hanging down at his side is a wicker basket, inside are three bottles of wine. He smiles widely upon seeing me, winks, fixes his amazing hair in the sexiest way imaginable, and welcomes himself inside without the need of an invitation.

Coming toe to toe, Tyler leans down and brushes a kiss over my surprised lips. "Missed you."

Um. Wowza.

My heart gives a wild thump.

"*Missed you more,*" I sign, watching Rob out of the corner of my eye. He hasn't moved an inch, but is viewing the exchange.

I can't believe they're here together. I'm not complaining one bit, but it would've been nice to get a heads-up.

A final peck to my forehead and Tyler goes about his business, not like a guest, but a resident who's been living here for years. He even remembers to kick off his Converse by the entry table.

Teeth sinking nervously into my bottom lip, I twinkly three-finger wave to Rob.

"Hey, babe." He steps into the house, crowding so closely that I have to tilt my head back to see his handsome face. Our feet brush. Per usual he's clad in jeans, motorcycle boots, a fitted t-shirt, and his leather riding vest that has his nickname, *Patriot*, patched on the breast. I'd ever use that name on him. Though, I do think it fits well.

"Hi." My cheeks heat, thighs pressing together from nerves, not arousal. Not that he isn't sexy or doesn't smell incredible. He wears cologne that would make any half-sane woman weak at the knees. The thing is, I can't believe he's really here. That we're doing this. Tonight is happening. Tyler and Rob have met a few times before, but we've never done this—powwow in my home. It's overwhelming. Downstairs in the dungeon, I'm the Domme, in charge, where I call the shots. Up here, it's a different playing field. We're equals, and I'm not sure how to cope with that. It doesn't bother me. Really, it doesn't. It's just... I'm kind of a control freak, and this is well outside my area of expertise. There's no manual on relationships, especially this type.

When I say nothing more, Rob cups my cheek in his big mitt, gentle heat seeping in, and brushes a tender kiss across my lips. I shiver despite myself. Another more solid kiss follows, lingering, sticky with fresh gloss. My eyelids shutter, and breath fumbles. Goosebumps prickle everywhere. Yet, with my hands clasped in front of me, I restrain myself from doing more. Now's not the time.

A body presses against my back, startling me enough to squeak into Rob's kiss. In response, he groans hot and heady. Strands of my hair are brushed to the side, and another set of lips feast on my neck— Tyler.

Oh, my... I melt to mush on the inside, reeling, feeling, indulging.

I'm officially sandwiched between two men for the first time in my life. And we're standing in the open doorway, putting on a dinner show for my neighbors. It's so perfect it almost feels like a dream.

"I think we need to eat food before we eat other things," Rob mutters, prying himself away from our kiss.

I nod dumbly in agreement as Tyler continues his assault.

Yep. Uh huh. He's right. We need to eat food. My food. It should be done by now. But first I gotta stop Tyler. And...I don't wanna. I want him to keep doing that... *Mmm... Right there.*

Drunk on his touch, my head lolls back, giving him better access, as Tyler's arm snakes around my stomach, joining us together. The outline of his erection presses against my spine.

In front of me, Rob scowls like a scary badass. Then, in a blur, he reaches out, grabs a fistful of Tyler's hair, and wrenches those luscious lips from my neck. Jesus, that shouldn't turn my crank like it does.

Keeping hold of our artist, Rob forces him to read his words. "Stop it, boy. We need to eat. You're the one who wanted to have this talk. So we're gonna talk." Statement received, Rob releases Tyler and folds his arms over his chest, waiting for... something.

Standing his ground, Tyler's palm splays across my belly. I look down to see those long, dexterous fingers staking an odd claim that makes my stomach go wonky.

"We can eat, Big Rob, but don't pretend you ain't liking this, too," Tyler provokes.

He isn't wrong. There's a definite banana shape running down the inside of Rob's pant leg. At the tip, a small wet spot has begun to bleed through. My Big Guy is one helluva pre-cummer, and I love it.

To avoid a possible showdown between my fellas when emotions are running high, I steer our focus where it should be—dinner.

Removing Tyler's hand, I scoot away and head for the kitchen. "Come on." I wave them forth, hoping they'll follow, not argue.

The sound of the front lock engaging is music to my ears. As is the *clunk* of Rob's boots being stowed.

I remove the manicotti and bread from the warm oven as both of my men join me. Somehow we silently perform our own personal kitchen dance like we've been doing it for years, not the first time. Tyler finds the corkscrew and opens a bottle of white and red wine. I'm a fan of both, as is he. To keep Rob happy, Tyler also retrieves the scotch from the cupboard above the stove before he pours us each a drink. As our artist shuffles about, Rob sets my four-person table with plates, forks, and the white cloth napkins he found in a drawer. That leaves me with barely anything left to do besides transfer the casserole dish filled with bubbling mozzarella to the table and plate the garlic bread. I was tempted to make a tossed salad tonight as well, as a lighter side, but Rob isn't a lettuce or spinach eater, and Tyler hates salads altogether—even the potato variety. What can I say? My men are wholesome foodies. Not rabbits. I know, you can't tell it by looking at either of them.

Everything in place, including the parmesan cheese and bottles of expensive wine, we take our respective seats. Tyler groans on impact, gripping the edge of the table as a potent wave of pleasure morphs his face for a good minute. Fascinated, both Rob and I watch him adjust to his sore bottom. Then, without any effort at all, the smooth dance in the kitchen transfers to the dining room. Back and forth, we take turns plating our own food before digging in without a word. We must have a lot on our minds, yet no idea how to broach the subject, so we don't. Instead, we eat in companionable silence, enjoying each other's company without obligatory chatter filling the space. It's cathartic in a way. Most nights I eat alone in front of the TV. Tonight, I don't have to. And I like that. I like it a lot.

Out of my periphery, I watch my men chow down. Tyler's refined and slow, each piece cut to the ideal size. The Big Guy doesn't bother with formal table manners. He roughly saws his manicotti in half with a fork and shovels the entire section into his maw like a caveman. I hate to admit it, but I find both men's eating habits charming. Having them here at the same time soothes something within me that I can't quite put my thumb on.

Stuffed to the gills, I shove my plate away, so I'm

not tempted to eat any more. It doesn't take long for Tyler to do the same. Rob finishes last, leaving very little for leftovers.

Hands folding in my lap, I sit and wait for someone to break the ice besides me. Thankfully, less than a minute ticks by before Tyler recognizes the growing discomfort and takes the initiative himself.

"I'm going to cut to the chase." He clears his throat and cards fingers through his hair. "This isn't working for me."

Wait. What?

Is he breaking up with... *us?*

Taking Tyler's announcement the same as me, Rob leans back and crosses his arms again, expression guarded.

This is not how I saw the night going.

"Go on," I encourage, trying hard not to die on the inside. Overreaction gets us nowhere.

"I think you both know this hasn't been working for a while now. That's why I wanted this dinner. Two days a week isn't enough. Not when I need more."

"Are you breaking it off with Ronan?" Rob interjects.

Tyler sits up straight, eyes blown wide. "What? *No!* Why would I do that?"

"'Cause it sounds like you are," Rob returns.

"I'm not. Why in the hell would I do that? I love her. I love you both. Why would I want that? *Shit!*" Tyler smacks his forehead and slips fingers into the front of his hair to fist. "This is coming out all wrong. I want us all to live together. *Here.* It's the best solution. My apartment's pointless since I barely spend any time there as it is. And my lease will be up the first of the month. I would like to make whatever this is more permanent. I know we haven't exactly spent a ton of time together, the three of us. But we talk constantly, and I think it would work in our best interests if we stopped dancing around what we want."

"I never said I wanted to live here, or with you," Rob growls, biceps tightening in protection mode.

"Are you saying you don't?" our artist tests.

"How's that gonna work, Tyler? We share the same bed? Ronan in the middle? What happens when I'm with my brothers and I fuck somebody else? What happens next, huh? Am I just supposed to come home, climb into bed, and pretend I didn't just get my dick wet in somebody else's cunt? When we'll all know, I did. It's bad enough dealin' with this issue with the way things are. It already feels like I'm cheatin'."

"But you're not. We talked about this. I understand," I cut in, not wanting him to beat himself up over something he can't exactly fix. He's already on edge enough as is.

Rob's eyes bore into mine, fierce and strong-willed. "You think I don't know it hurts you? That alone makes everything so much fuckin' harder for me afterward."

"I've *never* said anything like that." I toss my hands up, upset that he'd say such a thing. He can't put that on me. I've done nothing more than be supportive even if I don't like it.

"You don't have to. I already know," he argues.

"You *can't* know that."

"Well. I. Do. I think part of the reason I still get

sick is *because* I see your face inside my head right after I come. Let's be real. I'm fucked up. Beyond fucked up. Intimacy is and always will be an uphill battle for me. There's no way I could expect anyone to handle that day in and out. Even if I wanted to live here and be together that way, I couldn't. I've done the marriage thing twice, it didn't work. *This* wouldn't work. But, whatever you two choose to do I will fully support."

"We're not doing this without you," Tyler tosses in, clearly stricken by this upheaval of emotions.

Rob shakes his head, the cords in his neck taut. His jaw ticks. "Then you're not doing it at all, which is *stupid*. You can't let me put a damper on your relationship. We can't fix me. That doesn't mean you shouldn't be together."

Sitting forward, I slam my palms down on the tabletop. "Rob, that's not fair!"

"Life isn't fair, sweetheart. I didn't ask to deal with this shit. But I do. The last thing I want is y'all dealin' with it, too."

"You *can't* decide that for us. We love you for who you are. Messy crap and all." Why won't he get that through his thick skull? I've accepted his baggage from the beginning. That's not going to change now. Living together is scary as hell. But it's something I think could work. It would give us joy that I think we could all use a bit of. We care enough about each other that it might be worth the occasional bump in the road that comes along with any relationship. However, like with everything else in life, it takes hard work. Why is he giving up before we even get a chance to try?

"I know that. Which is why I *can't*. You think it gets bad now. Imagine what it'll be like when I do roll in after fucking some club whore, lipstick on my neck, smelling of pussy that isn't yours. What's that gonna do to you... to what we *do* have? Is it worth wrecking us? I don't fuckin' think it is. I'm not givin' you up. That's not gonna happen. I gotta deal with my own shit. There's no way I'm puttin' it on either of you. The cost is too damn high."

"Then you'll use me," Tyler pipes up outta nowhere, voice as smooth as silk.

Rob's face scrunches up. "Use you how?"

"The guilt shouldn't be there if we keep the sex inside our relationship. You can use me to fulfill whatever it is that needs fulfilled instead of those club whores," Tyler clarifies, shocking the hell out of me.

"You mean—" Rob begins.

"That you fuck me? Yes. That's exactly what I mean."

"Tyler—" I start. He puts his hand up to stop me. There's no way he can be serious. Sure, the thought excites me. But to actually go through with it is a huge step. Massive. This is a big deal, a major one. I'm not sure what to say, or how to feel. I'm kinda... just... wow... um...this is unexpected.

Slouching back in the chair, stunned, I let the moment unfold without interference. This is between them anyhow.

Resting his elbows on the table, Tyler glances between Rob and me as he speaks with admirable conviction. "I want this relationship to work with the three of us. If that means Rob has to have sex with me, I'm fine with it. I already like anal sex. Having a man I care about do it, instead of you, doesn't seem all that different."

"I'm not gay, and neither are you."

Rob's right. They're not. Just because you love anal penetration doesn't place you in the bisexual category like some might assume. You have to be attracted to the same sex for that to be true. Since when has either of my guys been into men? They haven't. I feel like I've wandered into some femdom, fantasy twilight zone.

Tyler isn't quick to give up. "I hear what you're saying, but I don't see why that matters when you're just looking for a hole to unleash on, control, and wreck. I love pain. You can hurt me, I'm gonna love it. In case you haven't noticed, I'm sitting on an ass that's the color of an eggplant, *and* I have a boner. Plus, you can spew all the degrading things you want, and I can't hear you." He taps the side of his head, grinning. "I'm deaf. Remember?"

Jesus. Tyler's erect and I'm getting turned on listening to them battle back and forth. What a messed-up bunch we are.

Rob cracks his neck from side to side, angrier than before. "I'm. Not. Gay. Even if you're okay with it, I dunno if I am."

"Why? Because I have a penis? What does it matter if I have a willing hole? Maybe it's not a vagina, but it works similar with lube. You won't even have to stretch me if you don't want. I like the pain. Hell, forget the lube, and I'll still love it! This is a much better solution and you know it."

It sounds too good to be true.

I squirm in my seat, hating myself for loving this

as much as I do.

"You have to be attracted to me to want me in there," Rob contends.

"Who says I *don't* find you attractive?"

"You're a straight boy."

"So?" Tyler shrugs. "I find your body appealing even if I'm more attracted to you on a mental level. Honestly, I could care less what's between your legs. Or your lack of feminine curves and breasts. Ronan has a dick too when she wants, and I love that. This is the best option for us. I want to live here with both of you. If that means I take it up the ass by someone other than Ronan, I'm fully on board with it."

"I don't think I could do it. I don't swing that way. I'm not attracted to men." The fire in Rob's eyes dies a slow death. Part of me wonders if he's trying to convince himself this could work. I know the bond he and Tyler share. It's different. There's no denying that.

"But you love me. You don't have to say it for me to know it's true."

"It's not the same," Rob half-snarls, upper lip curling.

"Are you saying you can't do it, or won't?"

The Big Guy sighs long and hard. "I'm sayin' I'm not sexually attracted to you. I've never been interested in men before. Any of them. Now you're askin' me to cross that line."

"For *your* benefit," Tyler simplifies.

"I know. *Fuck!* I *know*."

Our kind-hearted artist reaches over and squeezes my shoulder. "Ronan, you're quiet. What do you think about this?"

That's a good question. I'm still trying to decide if this is batshit crazy or brilliant.

Not wanting to interfere with their decision, I play Switzerland. "I think it's your choice to make. I'll support whatever you two decide."

"You're okay with me fuckin' him?" Rob asks in a way I can tell he wants me to insert my inner Domme into the mix, and make the choice for him. There are many cases where I could. This isn't one of them.

"If that's what *you want* to do, I am."

"It'll be under this roof. It's not the same as the club whores. It's gonna be right in your face." I knew it. The Big Man is trying to dissuade me... pressure me into putting my foot down and calling this whole cockamamie idea off. When in reality, as crazy as it sounds, it could work if he wants it to.

There's no way I'm going to be his scapegoat. "Tyler isn't a club girl. He's our partner whether you have sex with him or not. It's not the same."

"So, what you're sayin' is, hypothetically, you wouldn't be hurt if you walked in on me fuckin' him in our bedroom, if we all lived here."

Hell no. I'd love it. I can't exactly say that out loud when it might upset him, or sway his decision in one direction or the other. I'm trying my best to be honest, yet, supportive.

Poised, tone even-keeled, I reply, "As long as you sometimes let me watch, then I'm okay with it. There are a lot of rules that would need to be discussed before we agreed to a new living arrangement. Including having sex one on one without the other partner present—"

Rob throws up a palm, halting what I was about to

say. "Wait. Hold up. You would wanna *watch* us?"

Is the sky blue?

The grass green?

Do bears shit in the woods?

Lord have mercy, gay sex is some of the sexiest fucking on the planet. Who in their right mind wouldn't wanna see that action up close and personal? Woo wee, that shit is panty-scorching hotttttt—with six t's, not one. Can I get an *a*-two-dicks-are-better-then-one-*men*?

Subduing my visceral thoughts before they go awry, I do my best to keep Rob's jaw from hitting the floor any more than it already has. "I am a woman, who loves penis. So yes, watching two men go at it does have its appeal. Add in the fact that I love the two men in question, and I find it considerably more appealing." *Aka I could come watching you together*.

Rob throws his head back and drags both palms down his face. "Fuck!"

"You wanted the truth."

He stares at the ceiling. "It'd really turn you on?"

"Oh yeah." To the nth degree.

"E-even if I'm fuckin' him, not you." The poor guy is lost. He doesn't understand or doesn't want to. It's time to lay all the cards on the table since I don't think I'm getting my point across.

"Yes. If you haven't gotten the memo, I love cock, and I'm not ashamed of that. Whether it's having my own, or either of yours, I love them any which way I can get 'em. If that includes a little guy-on-guy action, then I'm totally on board. Only, if that's what my two guys want. This isn't about what I find hot. This is about what's healthy for us collectively. Do I believe you having sex with Tyler could help? Possibly. I don't know. It could make things worse. You could regress. It could cause a lot of problems. Or, it might be the answer for the club girl obstacle that's never done us any good. We didn't know you loved anal sex until we tested it out. But this is a bit different than that."

"If I agree to this, I'm not agreeing to let Tyler top me at some point. That's reserved only for you."

"I wouldn't expect that anyhow," Tyler replies. "This is strictly a you top, me bottom, arrangement."

"You're sure that wouldn't be a problem?" Rob double-checks.

A steady, mature nod. "I'm sure."

The Big Guy twists in his chair, giving our sexy masochist his full attention. "My dick is different than Mistress's."

Tyler snorts his amusement, smirking, eyes alight. "I know. I have one of my own."

"I'll be coming inside you, even with a condom, that's different than with Ronan."

I can't believe he just said that.

Oh. My. Wow.

Tyler cocks his head to the side, winking. "I know that, Dad. You don't have to treat me like a child."

"You're two decades younger than me, boy. I need you to think this through. A man with a whole lotta fucked-up anger issues, who's much older than you, will be pounding your backdoor. Hard. Not caring about your release or feelings."

"Believe it or not, old man, I understand. And we don't need to worry about condoms. I'm also fine with bareback. We both know we're clean."

Bareback... Cum... Creampie...

Holy Aphrodite! Is it a bazillion degrees in here or is it just me?

Trapping my hands between my thighs to keep them from doing whatever, I expel a shuddery breath, belly quivering.

Rob adjusts the apparent bulge in his pants, trying to be discrete and failing. "Yeah. I...Fuck. I dunno if I can be raw inside you... I can't believe we're debating this in the first place. What the hell are we doing? Why is this up for discussion?"

"This doesn't have to be decided tonight," I add, hoping I don't sound as breathy as I think. "We-we've got time to map everything out."

"If we don't talk this out now, I'm never going to have the courage to do it again."

I nod. "Fair enough."

"If, and that's a huge if, I can stomach this, I'll agree to moving in. My apartment is on a month-to-month lease anyway. If it doesn't, I think you should both still move in together without me."

"It'll work." Tyler's confident.

"Don't count on it." Rob's not.

"Does that mean this is a go?" I test, unsure of pretty much anything at this point. I assumed Tyler would put his foot down about us moving in together. That's the natural order of most relationships, even one as unique as ours. What I hadn't considered was the bisexual aspect. If I had it my way, everyone would be open minded and not care one iota about sexuality when picking their partner or partners. They'd care more about who they are and what attracts them. Not penis vs. vagina. As I've said before, I grew up in a free-to-be-you-and-me household. Not only were my parents hippies, but they were also swingers who had me late in life. They both passed six years ago within two months of each other. Mom went first from cancer. Dad, I think died of a broken heart. I'm an only child with no grandparents or close relatives of any kind, but I don't feel cheated by my lack of family. I was lucky to have parents who adored me and supported my profession. Heck, my mom's the one who first introduced me to the femdom lifestyle. As icky as that may sound to some, that was a large piece of my parents' relationship. Dad worshiped Mom in and out of their bedroom. Just like Tyler and Rob worship me.

A pregnant silence descends upon us as Rob ruminates over his decision, which is his and his alone to make. Tyler may have opened the can of worms, but it's the Big Guy who has to put the lid back on or set those worms free. Either way, I'm confident this will work out for the best.

Not wanting to waste my time sitting idly by, I redd up the messy table and stow the leftovers in the fridge. Tyler joins in by rinsing the dishes in the sink and placing them in the dishwasher.

Once finished, he cuffs a hand around my upper arm and draws me close, face-to-face.

"*I hope I didn't screw things up,*" Tyler signs, worry etched in his brow.

Smiling kindly to ease his concern, I lean a hip against the counter. "*It was kind of you to offer, no matter what Rob decides. As long as you did it for the right reasons and you're truly okay with it.*"

"*I am.*"

"*Have you thought about this before?*"

"*Wanting him to use me for relief?*"

"*All of it.*"

Tyler dips his head in acknowledgment. "*Yes. I didn't come here tonight with my head in the clouds. I know it'll be hard work syncing our lives under one roof. But I can say for certain that I hate going home to an empty apartment every night for no good reason.*"

Amen to that.

"*I see your point and feel the same way. Being alone sucks when the two men you want to spend your time with live in the same town.*"

"*Exactly. There's enough space here for all of us to live together without feeling overcrowded. If Rob can get past his issues, I think I could help him in a way you can't.*"

"*I do, too. Maybe.*" I shrug. Perhaps we'll be lucky. Perhaps we won't. Only time will tell. Where's a magical crystal ball when you need one? The waiting game sucks.

"*What other choice is there? To let this go on for years with no resolution? When I'm here, willing and able. It's not that far of a stretch if you think about it. People who know about our relationship already assume I'm bisexual. And considering people's stereotypes, they view me as a bottom. 'Cause by society's warped standards, Rob isn't the type. As if there's a type of man who's into anal versus not.*" Tyler rolls his adorable eyes, sporting a half-cocked smirk.

"*A ton of my fans assume I'm gay because I'm the*

deaf artist who paints erotic scenes. I accepted that years ago. I'm comfortable in my sexuality, whatever that might be. Labels are for soup cans. Not people... If I had a shitty childhood like Rob did, then I might feel differently. But I have a gay brother whose parents threw a coming-out party for, including a drag queen and go-go boys."

That would've been fun to attend. I love drag shows and go-go boys as much as the next woman. Can you say yum?

"I love that you own who you are. That's one of the million reasons I love you."

Stepping into Tyler's bubble, I wrap my arms around his middle, and lay my cheek to his chest. The *lub-lub* of his steady heartbeat centers me in a way nothing else can. Returning the hug, warm and protective, he builds our own Tyler-Ronan cocoon where nothing can harm us. We don't need to say anything when our minds are already a jumbled mess of what ifs.

Time passes at a snail's pace as Tyler's unique scent of fresh laundry detergent, paint, body wash, and vanilla keeps my brain from overreacting. Rob hasn't said anything yet. If we push, it's unfair. Patience truly is a virtue. One I'm not the fondest of at times like this.

A throat clears once.

Then a second time.

"Guys?" Rob's tone is strangely calm as I peek around Tyler to see the Big Guy standing at the entrance to the kitchen, naked and fully aroused.

Damn! That's... *Damn!*

Look at that cock.

Those strong, muscular legs.

Colorful tattoos.

Cum gutters—the special V where his thighs and hips meet. You know the place.

Flexing pecs.

Abs.

All of it.

I'm...

"Rob, w-what are you doing?" I croak before swallowing to dislodge the frog. Now it's Tyler's turn to swing his head around and whistle in approval at our brave man standing in the buff when we're still fully dressed. He must've thought it through, and talked the demons into their respective cages without my help. I'm more than impressed. I'm in awe.

Maintaining a safe distance from our Big Guy, not wanting to crowd him, I break out of the Tyler-Ronan bubble and give Rob the attention he's earned. Tyler's palm rests on the small of my back as he stands beside me, enjoying the super-hot view.

Crimson blots Rob's cheeks as he folds his hands together in front of him, anxiety surging off him in waves.

"I've decided I want this to work in some way, if we can." Staring at the floor, not at us, his toes curl under, the tendons in his feet drawing taut. I don't know why I find that sexy, but I do. I guess that's what happens when you're in love with two incredibly attractive men.

"What does that mean?" I ask, playing it cool.

"It means, I agree to Tyler's terms as a trial run."

I can't believe what I'm about to say. "You want to fuck him?"

"I wanna try and fuck him. Yes." My insides spasm at the conviction lacing Rob's words, and the slight nod he supplies.

I think I might've had a mini orgasm.

Keep it together, Ronan.

I flex my own toes as a distraction.

It doesn't help much when Tyler has taken to tracing designs along the top of my ass and lower back. Sometimes the smallest of touches have the biggest impact, and those fingers are turning me on for no apparent reason.

"Do you want me to give you the room to explore this? You can use the dungeon." It's a safe space for all of us. I think it would be the ideal spot for them to test the waters. If that's what they really want.

Rob looks up, locking eyes with mine. "I think it'd be best if you're with us."

That's impossible.

"I can't control the scene, or participate in it, Rob."

"You're gonna need to do both."

Tucking arms across my breasts, I shake my head vehemently. "No way. I don't control when you screw your club girls, nor am I ever there. This isn't about me. This is about *you* getting what *you* need."

"Right. And I need both of you." He's way calmer than I am. And Tyler has yet to say a word.

"At different times you do, but never at the same freaking time. Say I am part of it, how does that make it any different than if you used me instead of him? It doesn't." This is insane. What's he thinking?

"You're my Mistress. *You* fuckin' own me. *You* have the power. Our emotional connection is far too great for my brain to cope with using your body for personal gain. Power shifts fuck with my head, but that doesn't mean you can't be present. I don't see how that'll change anything if you are. You're the top to my bottom. When we all sure as hell know I need a bottom to top as well. Havin' both in the same place at the same time might be the key. Who the fuck knows unless we try?"

I get what he's saying... sorta. We've spent months and months figuring out a way to keep everything in their own distinct compartments, not mash them all together. Not once has he asked to, or have we considered him topping anyone during a scene, besides me, and we all know how that turned out.

"How is me helping you top Tyler going to work? Your need to fuck and our relationship are separate. To you. To our dynamics. You have to do this on your own, without me. There's a difference between true consent, and consent when you feel it's your only choice to make someone happy. I'm not interested in the latter. Your consent must be for *you*. Not me. Not Tyler. This isn't a cheesy porn script where you're talked into bein' a bi guy for your horny girlfriend to watch. I love you no matter what. This is real life, Big Man. Real consent, not the illusion of it." Gaahh! I wanna throw my hands up and storm from the room. I want to tell him I can't do this because I'm scared out of my mind—for him. He isn't taking baby steps. He's diving headfirst into shark-infested waters. We don't do that. Heck, I don't even do that with clients. Why would I want to try with my lovers? Babies walk before they run. You sink before you swim. It took us forever to make love, since we can't actually fuck or he loses his mind. This isn't a race. It's a damn triathlon that he's treating like a simple jog around the block.

Rob massages his forehead, sighing. "This isn't false consent, babe. It's real. I thought about it. What this could mean. What this could fix. I'm a realist, and this is our best option. We'll take it slow. But I'm gonna need you there to do it. You're our Mistress. Your support is gonna make this transition a helluva lot easier. You keep me sane, as does Tyler. Without one, I dunno if I can fuck the other. Ya got me?"

That's not all that reassuring.

"What's goin' on inside your head?" That's what matters most. Not some false bravado, if that's what it is. I can't tell.

He grins, warm and sweet, the mature lines that accentuate his eyes crinkling. "For once, it's not screamin' in sin. Much."

Well, I didn't expect that.

"That's a good sign."

"It is. See, I know what I'm doin', babe."

"If you're sure..." *I'm not.* "How do you want to proceed?" *This is crazy.*

"I think we should use the living room." Tyler finally adds his two cents, adjusting the bulge in his jeans.

"In the living room?" Fighting a grin, I knock my shoulder into Tyler's playfully. *"Why not my bedroom? Or the dungeon?"*

"If it doesn't work out, we don't want bad memories in those places," he reasons.

Touché.

Smart man.

"Good point." Rob nods, pivots on his heel, dick

swaying, and marches to the living room like a man on a mission.

"*He's not taking this seriously enough,*" I sign to Tyler, not ready to join Rob just yet.

My adorable artist faces me and arches a brow. "*Did you ever think that maybe you're taking it too seriously?*"

I scowl. "*This isn't a small thing. It is serious.*"

Tyler pecks my forehead. He's trying to pacify me. I can tell. Men. "*Maybe Rob doesn't want to view it that way anymore. Maybe he wants to view me like he would any of the other whores he screws; like I'm nothing more than a hole that he gets release from. There's no way he spends hours contemplating whether or not he's gonna screw some random pussy. There's a void that needs filled, so he fills it. Like an itch that needs scratched. You don't think about that itch for ten hours. You scratch the damn thing.*"

I hate when they make more sense than I do. Admitting defeat stings.

"*Why are you two the calm ones and I'm the one freaking out on the inside, even though I find this stupidly hot?*"

"*Because you love us and want what's best for us. I'm comfortable in my desires and can see this for what it is at face value. I'm not in Rob's mind to know for sure, but men don't think like women do. We don't overanalyze everything. We're black and white. I saw a problem and offered a possible solution. Rob put up his defenses like he always does, then let them down long enough to weigh the pros and cons on a base level. We care about one another.*

We want this to work. The whores are an obstacle. As men, we see that. There are no gray areas. It's cut and dry. You're the only one seeing this in Technicolor, sweetheart. We're using this as a means to an end."

Fine.

They're adults who can make their own choices. If this ends up blowing up in my face, I'm going to be the one picking up the gory pieces. They'd damn well better be on the same page, because I hate nothing more than preventable heartache. Why do you think I avoided relationships for the better part of my adult life? To escape the inevitable misery when it didn't work out. That's also why I've never lived with anyone. Not even a roommate. It's also why I don't have many close friends, aside from Kendra. It's a form of self-preservation. I might've grown up with excellent parents, but kids are cruel when said parents are different. Adults are far worse when you tell them what your kinks are, and they don't even attempt to understand. That's why I don't judge any of my kinksters. They can't help what they get off on. Trust me, if I preferred vanilla sex I would've settled down ages ago.

I'm deflecting again, aren't I?

Yup. I'm a pro at that.

Closing my eyes, pushing every ounce of stress out of my mind, I clear my thoughts and prepare for the next step in becoming, or not becoming a polyamorous partnership. It could go one of two ways. How Rob handles tonight will be the judge of that.

A final soothing breath and I'm ready to proceed.

I reopen my eyes.

"*You okay?*" Tyler hasn't budged.

"*Let's do this.*"

"*You're sure?*"

"*Are you sure? You're the one crossing the line. Not me.*"

Pressing his lips together to prevent himself from smiling, Tyler bows his head in a single reassuring nod.

Well then. What are we waiting for?

Taking the lead, since I am their Mistress, I exit the kitchen ahead of Tyler. He's hot on my heels as we enter the living room, where Rob's pacing back and forth in front of the ottoman that moonlights as a coffee table. His dick sways with each sure step, pecs bounce like a pair of Christmas hams. Glutes contract and release, accentuating those muscular dimples on either side that I wanna bite, mark, bruise. *Maybe later.*

Leaving Rob to his own devices, I take matters into my own hands. Since the Big Guy doesn't kiss or share intimacy with his lady friends, I presume he doesn't want that with Tyler either. Which means our artist needs to be prepped for penetration.

Turning toward Tyler, I two-finger point to the leather square he'll be lying on. "*Whenever you're ready, take off your clothes, and lie over the ottoman, ass up, chest flat on the top. Did you prep before you came?*"

"*Don't I always?*" He winks all smiles and charm, not nervous in the least. If anything, I'd say he's overcome with excitement.

"*Good. You thought ahead.*"

"You have a habit of sticking something in me every time I see you. I'm a Boy Scout, I come prepared." The smart-ass offers a two-finger solute, ice-blue eyes alight with humor.

"I'm pretty sure anal douching isn't offered as a troop patch."

"Maybe it should be. It'd be all the rage for the gay/bi boys."

I chuckle, trying hard to stay on track and failing. *"You're an idiot. Stop signing and get naked. I wanna see that cock. Is it hard for us?"*

"It hasn't gone down since before you opened the front door."

I figured as much. It's not like it's easy to hide in a pair of skinny jeans.

Giving Tyler the space he needs to undress, I take a quick trip to the laundry room's supply cupboards to grab a fresh bottle of strawberry-flavored lube, a new dildo, both of my men's collection of plugs, and a towel for easy cleanup. Returning to the living room, my naked men are standing, facing each other—observing. I pause my approach to give them time to appreciate the other's body. Rob's slack jawed staring at Tyler's pierced prick. At least he's still hard, so that's a good sign. If he wasn't this might not work. And I really hope it does, for all our sakes.

"Do you like what you see?" I address the Big Man.

Hands fisted at his sides, he shrugs a singular shoulder. "His dick's bigger than I thought it'd be for his size."

"Because he's thin?"

"Yeah. He's nicely hung."

"So are you," I remind.

The Big Guy grumbles the affirmative.

He's quite the charmer, isn't he?

Seeking instruction, Tyler glances in my direction, cool, calm, and collected despite his rosy cheeks from Rob's compliment.

Shoving all the goodies I'm carrying into one arm, I do my best to sign without dropping anything. *"Present your ass."*

If Rob thinks Tyler's cock is impressive, he's in for a treat. Tyler has much more to admire.

Being the perfect sub, our masochist turns around and there it is... that dark indigo bottom and wrecked back. The whip lines tell the beautiful tale of unconditional love that only his Mistress could create. The marks he bears leave me frozen in awe as a deep sense of adoration and pleasure bubbles in my chest. I did that. Those are from me. The hickies and bites on his neck are partially healed, but that posterior is the true art. The creamy notebook in which I write my sincerest love letters in a language that only Tyler and I can appreciate.

My bruised man peeks over his shoulder, eyes only for me. I grin softly, soaking up the moment. *"You're stunning."*

He takes my breath away.

"I love you." Tyler returns an equally tender smile that touches me in places nobody's hand ever could.

"Love you more. Now over the ottoman and spread your cheeks for me."

No words are spoken as he assumes the position, ready and willing.

"Why don't you sit and watch?" I gestured to the couch with the jut of my chin, hoping Rob will take a load off. He needs to experience this. See it all firsthand, so his brain doesn't get a chance to lie to him. If he wants to cross the line of no return, there's no reason to rush.

Without argument, he takes the middle spot on the sofa that's directly across from where Tyler's splayed.

Kneeling next to the ottoman, I dump the pile of good times on the floor beside me and grab Rob's medium-sized plug first. If he's going to penetrate our artist tonight and wants me to stay, he's going to do it my way. I toss it and the strawberry lube into his lap, careful not to hit his package.

"Go on. Put it in."

Rob blindly grips the end of the toy as he stares, transfixed on Tyler's exposed hole. Stomach flat, cheek pressed against the cool leather, fingers prying those marred globes apart, Tyler's dick points straight to the floor, a buffet waiting to be consumed.

"You want me to wear a plug when I fuck him?"

"I do."

Not wasting any time, Rob props one foot up on the couch for leverage, rises partway off the seat, and lubes the plug and his entrance before popping that bad boy in without missing a beat. I'm impressed. There's no resistance. No twinge of worry. No anxious behavior. Only compliance that has me wanting to fuck that pretty hole until he's ready to burst out of his skin.

Satisfied with the Big Guy's unwavering focus, I shoot out my upturned palm for him to return the lube. He does as he re-seats himself, legs spread, cock jutting toward the ceiling, balls resting on the couch.

A small shudder works its way through his body as he watches me drizzle a fair amount of liquid down the crack of our sexy masochist's ass.

Tyler emits a feather-light moan, goosebumps sprouting across his backside. I spank one bruised cheek then the other, to show Rob firsthand our guy isn't fragile. Upon impact I get my desired outcome—Tyler cries out, his fingers sinking deeper into marred flesh. I maintain my position at his side, not wanting to obscure Rob's view as I plant a nice juicy bite into the meat of his ass. Warm skin caves under pressure as a flood of endorphins intoxicate me. *Yes.* This is what I needed. Eyes sliding closed in pure ecstasy; I bask in his clean taste, the broken wails of bliss, and excited shivers that overtake him. How could Rob never want this? How could anyone not? Tyler's the embodiment of perfection. Any Mistress's ideal submissive.

Teeth sawing, nibbling, marking, I draw a finger down our man's crease, spreading the lube where it needs to be. Around and around I circle that hungry little bud before poking my digit into the center, breaching the outer ring to delve inside. Our artist's asshole hugs me tight as I glide in and out of his slick heat. From the couch, Rob rumbles like a caged animal waiting to break free. Watching, his expression intense, he chews his bottom lip and wraps a fist around his steel pole. Stroking it roughly, a bubble of pre-cum pools at the slit. With his thumb he spreads it around, using the silky wetness as his own personal lube.

This is insanely hot, and we've barely started. I pray this goes as planned. That he can handle it. A freak-out midfuck would be a disaster. But I don't want to baby him either. If he's made up his mind, then I'm not going to press any further.

Hole loosening, body going pliant under my direction, I unlatch my teeth and make eye contact with Tyler. Whose face is a thing of ecstasy-infused beauty—cheeks flushed, lips swollen, eyelids heavy, a sheen of sweat glistening on his forehead.

"You doing okay?" I double-check to be sure.

"Yes," he croaks.

"Are you ready?"

A small nod and shuddery exhale.

Perfect.

Adding a second finger, I watch my man's expressions contort from sharp, desired pain to bone-melting pleasure. That's exactly what I want to see. Tyler's body submitting to this moment. To the change in our relationship. I think it's time.

Slipping from his slack entrance, I back away from the scene to let Rob take the reins. There's nothing more I can do here. This is on them. I've done my duty.

Taking a seat on a wingback chair that flanks the sofa, I wait for our Big Man to take the initiative. I don't have to wait long. Cupping his knees, Rob scoots forward on the couch, inching closer to the hole that awaits him.

The naughty part of me wants to sit here with my legs crossed, clit throbbing, while I spout filthy things to encourage Rob. Just to turn the heat up to the next level. My heart's already on the verge of beating out of my chest, high on anticipation. Tyler's pleading eyes don't make this any easier for me. I'm used to stepping in and controlling the show, but this isn't my show to run. It's the Big Man's.

A minute passes before Rob slips closer. Another soon follows with no progression. By the time we reach the five-minute mark, I'm wondering if he's too caught up in his head to proceed. By six, I'm questioning my motives and if I should be doing more, even though in my gut, I know what I'm doing is the right thing. At seven, Rob expels an emotional breath and kneels behind Tyler. My pulse skyrockets at the marvelous sight. I can't believe this is going to happen.

Rob sets a single palm on Tyler's bottom, and I shake my head at our artist to keep him quiet. We don't want his moans to scare the Big Guy away. A tiny nod is Tyler's silent compliance.

Another palm joins in... barely touching.

A low, primal growl vibrates in our Big Man's chest.

Tyler's eyes tip back into his skull, nostrils flaring.

Testing the waters, Rob's fingers press into the bruised skin where he watches the colors change beneath his fingertips. Loving this too much, Tyler smashes his lips together to stifle a moan as a fresh batch of goosebumps sprout down his frame. I squirm in my seat, anxious to see what they do next. The only sound to be heard is Rob's harsh breaths as he traps his tongue between his front teeth, concentrating on the hole that beckons him, to come play, as it clenches and unclenches in time with Tyler's respirations.

"Damn," he husks, gripping his erection and aiming it at its desired destination. He shifts closer, knees digging into the plush rug. A subtle tilt of his hips and that pre-cum-drenched head kisses Tyler's entrance. A pleased sound emanates in his throat, Adam's apple bobbing on impact.

Lord Almighty, I don't think I've seen anything this hot in my entire life.

I slip a hand under the hem of my dress to stroke a finger up and down my smooth pussy lips.

Rob looks over, watching, waiting. To give him a better view, I tug my dress up, exposing myself from the waist down. Spreading my thick thighs, I draw a foot up to rest on the seat, relax my head against the chair back, and blow him a mischievous kiss. *That's right, babe, I'm turned on, too. Go on. Put that cock in our man's ass. Light his channel up. Make him cry out your name.*

Somehow reading my dirty thoughts, Rob secures Tyler's slender waist in one hand as he uses the other to glide inside our artist in a single flawless motion.

"Fuck!" he roars, throwing his head back, balls deep in that glorious tight heat.

Holy mother!

He did it!

I push two fingers into my cunt, wanting to join in on the action any way I can.

Tyler releases his cheeks to grip the top of the ottoman.

"Mistress," he mouths, a tear leaking out of the corner of his eye.

I know what he seeks.

"Go ahead." I nod in concession. There's no need for him to hold back any longer. Not when they're connected in the most intimate way possible.

Now free to make as much noise as he desires, Tyler sets loose a string of guttural moans as Rob digs his fingers into either side of our man's hips, the ink in his forearms shifting under strain. For half a second his forehead creases, deep in thought, before he unleashes the sexiest growl known to mankind and begins to fuck Tyler like a beast. There's no preamble. No more testing the waters. No making sure his partner's ready. Rob goes for it, raw, brash, and hot as Hades.

On violent repeat, he slams into that willing hole, the filthy clap of skin coming together echoing off the walls. Reading our masochist like a book, he spanks him hard, setting off another round of ecstasy-laden wails.

That's it, baby. Keep it up. Make him squeal.

My pussy clamps around my plunging fingers. If they keep this up, I'm gonna come a dozen times before they finish.

Another crack on Tyler's ass, more forceful than the last, leaves my poor submissive clawing at the leather, head thrashing back in forth—completely wrecked and desperate for more.

"That's right, boy." Rob drags his blunt nails down that perfectly marred back, amping both of their pleasure. Just as those punishing fingers reach the seam of Tyler's ass, his eyes burst wide searching for me, ready to combust.

I shake my head, refusing to give permission.

Not yet.

Worry steals across his sweaty face, as he emits a shuddery cry of defeat. I grin at his discomfort even if I shouldn't. My artist has more staying power than he gives himself credit for. He can endure. Rob has stamina that would make most men jealous. He should enjoy the ride while it lasts. And what a ride it is.

Rubbing my clit in time with the Big Guy's thrusts, I chew the inside of my cheek, trying hard not to get there too fast. It's not exactly fair if I climax so quickly when I forbid Tyler from doing the same.

Getting into it more than I thought possible, Rob pulls out, stands up, shoves our man's feet together using his own, and repositions himself so that he's straddling them. Lowering into position, one foot flat on the ground, the other perched on the ottoman, he forces his dick back inside from a pile-driving angle. Pressing a hand to Tyler's left shoulder, he grips a fistful of our masochist's hair with the second.

Yanking his head back, forcing my submissive to look him in the eye, Rob hammers into that tight, hungry rim. "Such a good slut, takin' my dick up your tight pussy."

"Yes." Redness rims our stunning man's eyes.

"You like it when I fuck your boy cunt?"

"Y-yes." Tears leak down his cheeks, his slightly parted lips, puffy from self-abuse.

"Tell me."

God, yes, tell him. *Tell him*! I'm gonna come. They're gonna make me explode. Dipping fingers into my wetness, I spread it around my clit and rub it fast, so turned on I'm going crazy.

"I... I love it when you... I... Rob!"

"You don't get to come, boy."

"I..." Tyler trembles from head to toe, trying hard to obey.

"I'm poundin' that prostate good, aren't I?"

Oh, yeah, you are. Fuck it harder. Tear that sexy ass up.

"Yes!"

"You wanna come with my dick up your pretty pussy?"

"*Please... I.*"

Rob scowls, wrenching our masochist's head back another centimeter, forcing his spine to bow. "No!"

A steady stream of pleasure-induced tears fall.

"Mistress!" Tyler begs, and that's all it takes. My own back bowing, eyes locked on my delicious men in action, I come, and I come, and I come in a torrent of white-hot ecstasy, calling out their names.

The world fades to black for half a second before refocusing on Rob, who has paused mid-fuck to watch me ride the wave of toe-curling bliss that they created with their dirty mouths.

"That was hot, babe." He smirks, then resumes his potent onslaught.

"You're both hot," I pant, drawing lazy circles around my clit. She's already primed for round two, so it doesn't take long for a second orgasm to take hold. Followed by a third, and a fourth, leaving me a trembling mess of boneless goo.

Yet, they carry on.

Fucking.

Connecting.

Sweat coating their bodies.

Muscles tensing with each thrust.

Hoarse moans pour like golden spun honey from Tyler's soul as Rob owns his pleasure.

Hooded eyes, floating in a sea of endless lust, beg

me to put him out of his misery, to give in and let him finish. But I can't. It's not time. I'll know when it is, and we're not quite there.

"Mistress," he breathes.

"She's not gonna save you, boy. Your slutty pussy is mine right now."

"I... I can't." Tyler's teetering on the edge. So close, yet so far.

"You will. Or we won't do this again. You readin' my lips? I won't wreck your boy pussy again if you come before me. And you want that, don't you?"

"Y-yes."

"Good."

Satisfied by Tyler's admission, Rob releases his hair and repositions himself—chest to back, both knees perched on the ottoman, pelvis cradling ass. Stuffing his face into our artist's neck, he runs his hands along Tyler's arms until he reaches his fingers and slots his own through. Then he places them above their heads, pressing them into the ottoman as he draws back his hips, leaving just the tip of his cock inside. Unleashing a wild grunt, Rob punctuates his full-body thrust with a burst of strength that forces both of their asses to jiggle on impact and the leather to groan.

Face down, our masochist cries out for more.

Heeding his call, Rob does it again and again, thighs contracting, shoulders flexing as he jackhammers our partner's hole into submission.

"Fuck! I'm gonna come." He stills halfway out. Then it happens. One final plunge, burying himself to the hilt, and his face contorts as he fills our masochist with jets of warm, salty cum. Knowing what's happening, Tyler's own dick explodes without permission, spraying my rug in ropes of semen. Screaming against the leather, he shatters into a million pieces.

They did it.

My men... they freaking did it!

I'm not sure how to feel right now. My heart's beyond full, it could burst.

Swallowing thickly, I try my darndest to keep the welling tears at bay. One sneaks through, and I swipe it away with the back of my hand before they notice. It's not often I cry from sex. And I've never gotten this choked up from watching a scene. I'm just so proud of both of them. They did it. This changes everything.

Not wanting to interrupt their post-coital glow, I stay quiet in my chair, and return my dress to its ladylike station.

Ousting a sated groan, Rob rolls off Tyler and deposits himself on the floor, face up, between the ottoman and my chair. His dick still hasn't softened. The remnants of cum slide down his shaft, pooling in the sparse hair at the base. I wanna lick it up, but think better of it. We don't know where his head's at right now. It could be playing catch-up, on the verge of purging.

He tucks an arm behind his head, showing off that massive bicep without even trying. "Damn. That was..."

When he doesn't finish his sentence, fear begins to creep in.

Please don't say this was too good to be true. That he's going to relapse. It wouldn't be the first or tenth time. I shouldn't expect this to be any different. If anything, I should expect it to be far worse. It's not every day you experiment with a man. I... I should probably go get a trash can just to be safe.

Scooting to the edge of the seat, Rob reaches up and cuffs a hand around my calf on its descent to the floor. Our eyes collide. I lick my lips. He repeats the action. Tyler rolls onto his side, remaining on the ottoman. Nobody says a word. And it's strange because we don't need to. The warmth that radiates through our connection chases my woes away. It's odd, really. I've never felt anything like it.

With the simple lift of his chin to me, then Tyler, our Big Guy calls to us, and we follow. I'm the first to stretch out on the floor beside him, laying my cheek on his pec. Rob's arm surrounds me, tucking me to his side. I throw a leg over his and trace designs down his abs, to the drips of cum, that I massage in with my fingertips. On the opposite side, Tyler mimics my pose, palm lying on Rob's sternum close to where his heart resides. We stare at each other for a long beat, across the short distance, then lean in. Lips brushing at first before our tongues join in on the sweet, soul-tethering caress. Soft and slow we kiss, savoring the quiet moment when everything is right in our world.

"That's it," Rob softly rumbles his encouragement. "We should've been doin' this for fuckin' years. I wish I would've known it could've been like this. We've wasted so much time."

Yes. We have.

I can't believe this is real.

A tear I can no longer hold captive falls to our Big Guy's chest.

He combs his fingers through my hair as Tyler deepens our kiss which speaks of love and commitment, of truth and purity.

"We're going to move in together. You're it for me."

That we are.

The three of us against the world. Forever.

This is the happiest moment of my life.

The end...
Not quite...

EPILOGUE

FOREVER IS WHAT YOU MAKE IT

One year later

Sitting on my couch, feet propped up on the leather ottoman, ankles crossed, wearing cotton shorts and a tank top, I give Michael, The Naked Submissive, my undivided attention. We're finishing an interview with Tyler and me for his wildly popular vlog that focuses on facets of BDSM lifestyles. Staying true to his brand, he is naked, mostly, aside from a plastic cock cage. Seated beside him, operating the camera is his Master. Who Rob and everyone else, besides Michael, calls Judge. Evidently, he's an unofficial brother of Rob's motorcycle club.

"Ronan, do you need anything?" The Big Man calls from the kitchen where he's putting away dishes. He's the reluctant one of the bunch, who's avoiding vlog airtime at all costs. Tyler, on the other hand, is used to the public eye and welcomes it with open arms. That's why he's sitting beside me, interacting with our guests and the potential viewers.

Digging into the mindset of a ProDomme who's in an exclusive polyamorous relationship seems to fascinate Michael. That's one of the many reasons I agreed to this interview in the first place. We also have a few mutual connections, and I happen to be a fan of Michael's vlog and website. They're informative in a risqué yet intuitive in a way that most sites don't offer. The majority of BDSM vlogs I've seen are either clinically drab or pornographic. I appreciate that The Naked Submissive tightrope walks between both, which makes for great entertainment.

I fold my fingers through Tyler's that rest atop my thigh, as Michael shoots off another rapid-fire question. "You were saying earlier that last year your relationship took a positive turn you didn't see coming. Are you referring to the bisexual status of your men?"

Uncrossing my ankles to scratch my shin with a foot, I nod the affirmative. "I was. But we aren't fond of labels. Is anyone?"

"I'm not. Can you please elaborate for us?"

I can, but... Let's pray I don't go off on another tangent. I've done that twice already. Hopefully, he can edit part of my craziness out. The last thing I want is his viewers thinking I'm a know-it-all-nelly with less charisma than a tadpole.

Smiling despite my nerves, I keep my voice light and airy. "To some, you'd be considered a gay sex slave with a cage and plug fetish. That isn't who you are, though. You're a vlogger, a loving husband, a partner, friend, stepfather." Speaking passionately, my hand gets animated following along with my speech.

"People often get caught up in the labels that they forget those who practice any facet of the BDSM lifestyle are normal people, too, with a taste for the spicier side of life. We aren't the kink. It doesn't define us. It rounds us out. Drives us. And there's something freeing about that."

"So what you're saying is your men don't consider themselves bisexual?" Michael already knows this. We've discussed it before. I'm merely reiterating it for the masses.

I shrug, playing along. "We are what we are. We enjoy what we enjoy. Tyler derives mental and physical pleasure from submitting to both Rob and me in very different ways. If that makes him bisexual, then he's bi by society standards. But, by definition, bisexual means you're attracted to both sexes. When in Rob and Tyler's case, they're not attracted to other men."

"Only each other," Michael illuminates for his viewers, who'll eat this shit up. It's a common misconception in life that you're born straight, bisexual, transgender, or gay. As if those are the only options. People believe that, because it fits inside their little box of media-influenced understanding. They don't believe that you can one day wake up and find someone of the same sex attractive. They'll label it latent homosexuality, or whatever mumbo-jumbo bullshit that makes them sleep better at night. As you can tell I'm rather passionate about this particular topic. What can I say? When it comes to my men, there's nothing I care more about.

Tyler's the perfect person to add his insight. "Yes. You could say that. But it wasn't like that at first. I was the last resort for an issue that might've ruined our relationships, had it not been fixed. It wasn't until months later when I started to realize that I found Rob just as attractive as I do Ronan. By then we were already sharing a bed, a closet, bathroom, meals, date nights, sex... you get the picture."

"That was an emotional day for all of us," I add, reliving the moment in my head like it was yesterday.

"How so?" Michael asks, genuinely interested.

It's my turn to shed some light. "Tyler's always been open-minded. He claims it's due to his parents and artist mindset that gives him the edge. Maybe it is. But Rob's a different story. He's a tough nut to crack. So when Tyler revealed what he felt, I was thrilled for not only him, but for us. To celebrate, I made dinner that night. Let's just say—"

"Long story short," Rob interrupts from the other room, gruff and unenthused. "I was an asshole when they told me. Ended up goin' on a run with my club brothers for a week. Froze everyone out. It took some soul searchin' and a certain brother's ass kickin', before I could face my own truth."

"That you were attracted to Tyler, also?" Michael's giddy with glee. He's practically vibrating in his chair. Any second now he's gonna start clapping his hands and bouncing up and down. If that happens, his dick, trapped in that cage, will start flopping around. Which I'm sure his master would not appreciate. He's already tried to convince Michael to cover up a dozen times since the camera never shows that part of his anatomy. You think he cares? Nope. He's all about being authentic—true to his brand and lifestyle. I'm sure Judge has his hands full with that one. He's quite the firecracker.

"Somethin' like that. Yeah," Rob grumbles belatedly, hating this. If I hadn't put my foot down, this interview would've never happened to begin with, thanks to the Big Guy's disapproval, who said the internet didn't need to know our motherfucking business. Tyler and I convinced him that maybe someone might watch us, and realize there's nothing wrong with them and what they want. That maybe the same person would embrace their desires, not shun them like Rob's mom had. Bringing his mother into the mix was our saving grace.

Michael thumb points toward the kitchen where the chicken is hiding. "He's difficult to handle, isn't he?"

"Very," Tyler and I reply in unison, as we glance at each other, grinning from ear to ear.

Michael outright laughs, and we join in on the belly-rumbling merriment.

Judge smothers his own chuckle, ever the serious fella, as Rob curses up a storm from his hiding spot.

"That's a wrap," Michael announces once we've calmed. He dashes a finger beneath each eye and Judge cuts the feed.

"Thank you all for doing this. I'll make sure I send you the edited version for your approval before I publish," he adds.

Have I said how much I adore this man? He reminds me of Tyler in a lot of ways. Judge is a lucky Dom.

I grin, curling my legs onto the couch to drape partway over my man's lap. He cuffs both hands in the crook of my knees. "Sounds perfect. I enjoyed myself."

"I did too. My followers can learn a lot from you. You don't get to hear a ProDomme's point of view all that often."

"Most people think we're prostitutes," I half chuckle, turning in to cuddle my artist, cheek rubbing against his arm like an attention-starved kitten. We haven't had sex since early yesterday. The nympho in me is about to rip his clothes off and get down to business. Between the three of us, we never go a day without sex. Not one. If I'm tired, the guys make it a point to fuck while someone licks me to climax. If Rob's too worn out, we take turns giving him a blowjob. Then I top him to completion. If Tyler's busy working, we often invade his space to steal what we want, aka bow-chicka-wow-wow, when he's otherwise too occupied to think about sex.

"And most people think I'm forced into slavery with Master. Apparently, I have Stockholm syndrome." Michael rolls his eyes as his partner in question drapes a t-shirt over his sub's privates.

"You've been naked long enough," Judge scolds, giving Michael what could only be described as the eye.

Slipping into his role with ease, Michael drops his head forward, chin to chest, in absolute obedience. It warms my heart to witness in person. It's not often you get to experience the nuances of a relationship similar to yours up close and personal.

"If you don't mind me saying, I think you make an amazing couple," I compliment. They do. I could tell from the moment they walked in the door that they're well matched.

Michael blushes as Judge, the other silver fox present, bows his head out of respect. "I should say the same to you. I don't have the experience of a well-trained Dom, as you do. It's remarkable what you've created here, while still keeping your day job as a professional Mistress. It's impressive."

"Well, if you ever need any tips or help, call or email anytime."

"I'll have to take you up on that."

"May I ask a question?" Tyler inquires, pressing a kiss to the top of my head.

"Yes," Judge answers, sitting up straight, hand perched on his husband's thigh.

Tyler points his chin to Michael's lap. "How does one get into cages? Is there training involved? How did—"

"You're not wearing a cage," Rob interjects hostilely, sauntering into the living room pissed off, needing an outlet for that rage. He stops beside the couch closest to Tyler and repeats himself for our masochist's benefit.

"That's not up to you. That's Mistress's, choice. Not yours." Tyler's lips press into a thin line of displeasure.

"Boy—"

"Enough!" I clip.

Rob glares at our partner and then softens his expression when he addresses me. "He's not wearing a cage."

"Oh, really? And why is that?" He better have a damn good explanation for acting out in front of guests.

"Because I fuckin' said so."

Guess not.

He's marking his territory. At this rate, he might as well whip his dick out and piss on us.

You'd think after a year this macho man would have his shit together. He doesn't. It's better than it used to be. The sinner issues rarely emerge. But we put Rob in an uncomfortable situation today with this interview, and I knew he would lash out. It happens when he doesn't know how to express his feelings constructively. However, him asserting dominance over Tyler outside of the bedroom is one thing I cannot condone. We established our relationship hierarchy from the beginning. I'm their Mistress. I rule the roost. Tyler always prefers that. Rob has a habit of battling me for supremacy. I always win, of course, and this time will be no different.

Keeping calm, I turn my attention to our guests, ignoring the pink elephant in the room that has steam billowing from his ears. "Thank you so much for coming today. We should all go out sometime. But I have some—"

"I understand completely. You do what you need to do." Judge waves me off, winks knowingly, and gathers their belongings as Michael dresses. I unfold myself from the couch and stand to shake their hands before they depart with a promise to talk soon. Tyler walks them out without my delegation. I turn to Rob, clasp my hands behind my back, breasts heaving upward, and stare down my silver fox who's way out of line. If it were Tyler who acted up, I'd spank him with a paddle until he sobbed his need for release. Sadly, I can't resort to the same punishments. It'd be nice if I could.

"What do you have to say for yourself?"

"Nothing. Tyler doesn't need to be discussing cages with another submissive."

"Is that for you to decide?"

"Yes."

No. It's not. We decide new toys and everything else as a unit.

If he wants to be a stubborn butthole, two can play at that game.

Hooking my thumbs into my shorts, I shuck them and my panties to the ground where I kick them off. He eyes me like I'm a delicious candy buffet he can't wait to eat. Fat chance, with that attitude, that I'll let him sample the goods. I've learned that to teach Rob a lesson, you don't have to argue, since that usually does little to help the situation. You merely deny him something he wants. And that something is me. Next, I tear my tank over my head and discard it, pretending he isn't standing in front of me with an obvious boner.

Giving him my back, I face Tyler, who, by the subtle wink he offers, knows exactly what I'm up to. See, we're on the same page. He gets me. This isn't the first time I've had to put a certain someone in his place. He has a habit of trying to mark his territory, when it's unnecessary. For instance, at the grocery store last week he stuck his tongue down my throat in the bread aisle when he thought some biker he knows was checking me out. He wasn't. All the guy wanted was the wheat bread I was standing next to. But Rob couldn't see past his defenses. In a way it's adorable. In another, I want to throttle him. So I go this route instead. It's more fun for everyone involved.

Stepping closer to Tyler, I offer him an upturned palm, and he locks his hand in mine. Here goes nothing. Taking the lead, I escort our sexy artist to the bedroom down the hall, with Rob in tow. It's not like I expected him to sit idly by as I screw our masochist in the other room.

Stopping next to our king, four-poster bed, that none of us bother to make any more, I block Rob's view of Tyler the best I can, by standing in front of him. I don't make the best wall, considering they're taller than me by a lot. But I can't give him a front row seat to our kink show. Not when he's in trouble.

"Undress and position yourself against the headboard. Are you wearing your plug?" Signing in front of the Big Man when he knows we're up to something drives him insane.

As if on cue, Rob voices his aggravation. "Words. You know I don't like when you do that secret shit."

See. Do I know him or what?

Tyler snickers, able to read the broody butthole's lips from here.

I roll my eyes, doing my best to avoid smiling. It's futile when this is entirely too much fun. Hell, our entire life is chockful of it. Living together is quite the adventure. You never know where the next day will lead. Whether we're hanging with bikers at Nowhere, or attending a gala that showcases Tyler's art. Even down to the simple things like arguing over which show is better—Vikings vs. Game of Thrones, there's never a dull moment. Oh, and in case you're wondering, our house is an uneven split. Two for Vikings and one for Game of Thrones. You'll have to guess who chose what because I'm not going to tell you. It's a secret amongst lovers.

Not letting Rob deter him, Tyler focuses his energy on me. *"I am wearing my plug. Do I need to take it* out?"

"No. We're not doing that today. I have something else in mind."

Needing no further explanation, our super-hot partner undresses, going for speed, not sensuality. Once naked from head to toe, he crawls into the middle of our mattress, marked ass swaying for effect, before he positions himself against the headboard. Legs straight out, his pierced cock is ready to tango.

Following suit, I do the same crawl and ass sway, playing up my curves they love. Sitting on my feet beside Tyler, I draw a fingertip up the inseam of his thigh, ankle to balls. He shivers, emitting the tiniest noise from his throat.

"You ready for me?" I purr, licking my lips for show, wanting them primed and ready for what happens next.

"You gotta be fuckin' shittin' me," Rob growls from the end of the bed.

Out of the corner of my eye, I watch him grip the footboard hard enough his knuckles blanch. The wood groans under pressure. Now we're getting somewhere.

Throwing a leg over Tyler's, I straddle his calves. He grips the pillows on either side of him to occupy his wandering hands. When I'm in charge, he knows he can't touch without consent. I'm glad somebody recognizes their place.

To solidify Rob's mounting torment, I rotate my hips in a slow sensual motion, combing fingers through my silky curls. Back slightly arching, my bosom arcs toward the ceiling, rosy tips desperate to be sucked on. Hungry eyes sear through me, watching, feasting, evoking shivers, spurring me on.

Needing more, so much more, I inch my way closer to Tyler's waiting shaft. I moan, and my cunt spasms, anxious to be filled, to have her g-spot owned by that studded cock, ready to take it deep. I pass his knees, pussy lips grazing the tops of his thighs.

"Mistress," Tyler breathes, air punching from his lungs, pupils, already blown.

Cupping his stubbly jaw, I lean forward and trace his lips with the tip of my tongue, tasting him, savoring his flavor. A final swipe and I seal our mouths together, grasp that beautiful dick, and lower myself onto him painfully slow, taking my time, needing to feel every perfect inch.

Yesss.

That's what I needed.

This.

Us.

Him inside me. To reconnect. To be.

"Ronan," Rob rasps in broken desperation.

Hmm... someone's unhappy. I wonder why. Is the Big Man feeling a little left out? I bet he is.

Prying my lips from Tyler's, I glance over my shoulder. "Can I help you?"

"Why are you doin' this?" Rob's face is bright red. Someone took off his shirt and is busy playing with his nipples.

"Now why do you think?"

His jaw works. "Fuck. Okay. I was outta line."

"And?" Eyes on Rob, I cup the back of Tyler's head and lift a breast to his lips. Taking direction, he suckles my tit into his mouth, swirling and nibbling on the bud—driving me mad. I rock back on his cock, fucking it with mini-strokes. Just enough for us to feel amazing, but not enough to make me come.

"And? Why does there gotta be a damn and?" Somebody's still not getting it.

Arching a cynical brow, I wait patiently for him to stop fighting over nothing. He knows what he did was wrong. There are rules we follow in this relationship. He broke one. As their Mistress, it's my duty to punish them for stepping way outside our established lines. Where many women would yell at their partner for acting out, I choose a different tactic. One that works without creating an overdramatic episode that would leave us all upset. My way's better. It ends in orgasms. Which would you choose?

"Alright. I'm sorry. I could've handled it better."

See.

There's a method to my madness. It works like a charm.

All I ever ask if for him to own his actions and apologize accordingly.

Pleased it didn't take too long, I forgive his indiscretions as if they never happened, and give in to temptation. There's something I want, and I'm not afraid to take it. And that something is standing at the end of the bed, half-naked, ready, and more than willing.

"Good." I nod. "I'm glad we cleared that up. Now grab the lube. I want you inside my ass. I think I deserve a little double penetration today, don't you?"

Rob groans, palming his erection through his jeans. "Hell yes, babe. Hell. Fuckin'. Yes."

Indulging in a grin that reaches my eyes, I point to the nightstand, wanting him to hurry up.

"I expect you to come inside me, too." Lots and lots of cum. I want it leaking out of every orifice... There's no better feeling in the world than to own and be owned.

"Anything for you, sweetheart. Anything." He works the button of his pants free.

"All I want is you both. Forever. Like this." My soul couldn't have picked better mates.

Offering me a kind smile, Rob removes his jeans and boxers. "And that's what you're gonna get, baby. We're not goin' anywhere. Now let me find the lube. You've got some coming to do."

Amen to that.

Aren't I the luckiest Domme in the world?

THE END

AUTHOR NOTE

Fellow kink lovers,

Thank you so much for reading Marking My Men. I know this isn't a typical Bink story. But one day I was sitting in my living room talking book talk with Deb, and she started telling me I should write a book about a Domme. At first, I was skeptical. Sure, I had a partner in the past who I practiced a milder version of this lifestyle with, so I have firsthand experience. I just never thought I'd write a book with not only one submissive, but two. Much to my surprise, an hour after our discussion commenced I was convinced this was the book to write, after I'd finished the long and emotional Sacred Sinners MC- H.O.P.E. trilogy expedition.

At this point, after reading this kinky yet oddly sweet story, you're either left strangely satisfied, disgusted or a wonky combination of emotions. There's nothing I can say to you besides thank you for taking a walk on the ProDomme wild side. If anything, I hope you learned a thing or two. Maybe that this kinda book turns your crank. Or that it doesn't. Perhaps you're ready to write me off as an author. Or, you love me more for pushing the limits. Whatever it is, I'm glad you took this journey.

Happy Reading.

Peace,
Bink

Printed in Dunstable, United Kingdom